"My mot... was a softy...

He smiled, not at Janet but perhaps at some long lost memory of his mother. "A softy for injured birds and dumped kittens. I love her for it, but I won't let it kill her. She can't take in every sad case that comes along."

"Lucas, you'll kill her if you take this place away from her. She's going to give it her best shot, and so am I."

Lucas stared out over the lake and tapped his fingers against the railing. When he finally turned toward her, he gave her an odd look. "And so am I."

"What does that mean?" Janet had thought that he'd softened, but he would fight them all the way. And she had the sinking feeling he wouldn't fight fair.

Lucas touched the tip of a finger under her chin and lifted her head, his lips close. He smiled again, dark eyes flashing mischievously. "Let's just let it be a surprise."

Marcella Thompson has lived in various parts of the United States but always came back to what she calls her mountains in Arkansas. Finally she decided to stay. She and her husband, Glenn, raise blueberries during the summer, and Marcella writes in the winter. They live on a lovely piece of land near Fayetteville with a collection of dogs and cats, all of which she says are "strange and special in their own way."

Bed, Breakfast & Bedlam was inspired by a dear friend of Marcella's who regularly abandoned institutional nursing for friends—usually elderly friends—who were seriously ill.

Books by Marcella Thompson

HARLEQUIN ROMANCE
2802—BREAKING FREE

Bed, Breakfast & Bedlam

Marcella Thompson

Harlequin Books

TORONTO • NEW YORK • LONDON
AMSTERDAM • PARIS • SYDNEY • HAMBURG
STOCKHOLM • ATHENS • TOKYO • MILAN

ISBN 0-373-02975-6

Harlequin Romance first edition April 1989

For Liz
who makes the world a little brighter

PROLOGUE

JANET GALLEN sat in the nurses' lounge of the University Medical Center, her tired feet bared and propped up on a scarred coffee table, a copy of *Mother Earth News* in her lap. She heaved a lengthy sigh and wiggled her toes, staring at them thoughtfully, her deep blue eyes unblinking.

In the three months since that lunch in the hospital cafeteria—when Jack had told her he was through with his residency and through with her—she had changed, and definitely not for the better. Three months of looking up every time a door opened, staying at home nights—so she could tell him to buzz off just in case he changed his mind and decided to call—was for the birds. Jack was in Houston, Texas, by choice. She was in Little Rock, Arkansas, by default. And to make matters worse, everyone at the hospital kept saying, "You should have known better than to fall in love with a dermatologist." These were, of course, the same people who had told her all along what a perfect couple they were. She'd finally realized she couldn't stay at the Med Center any longer.

It was time for a change—a drastic change—in her life. Twenty-six was too young to be pining endlessly over the spilled milk of broken dreams. That thought brought her up straight. *Spilled milk of broken dreams?* Lord, she was beginning to sound like what's-her-name in *Wuthering Heights*. She poked at the wisps of sandy-red hair that refused to stay confined by her nurse's cap and looked at the ad she'd circled in the magazine.

Employment and Labor Exchange
Stubborn old woman determined to keep her home, looking for ambitious young woman to share in business. Must be qualified nurse, able to do cooking, cleaning, general repairs. Mostly need someone who likes old folks. Room and board, hard work, share in profits, if any. Apply at Crow's Rest on Beaver Lake, Rogers, Arkansas.

Janet couldn't imagine what the woman had in mind, but it sounded interesting. As long as she was going to make a change, it might as well be a *big* one. When you started sounding like a Victorian governess, it was definitely time for the Big Change. Besides, while surgery was her first love, geriatrics was her second. Being around old folks at this point was certainly preferable to being around young men. She put on her shoes, poked at her hair some more and went to make the call.

LUCAS McNAIR shoved files into his briefcase, anxious to begin the weekend. Anxious to get away from the human wreckage with which he dealt all week. When Lucas had taken the appointment as administrative law judge, he'd thought he could make a difference. Instead, he found himself bogged down in the same red tape he'd fought for years in private practice. So many people in so much need and so little he could do.

He was looking forward to his upcoming month's leave. He was going back home, to the mountains, to fish and sail and convince his sixty-eight-year-old mother that it was time she moved to a retirement home in Little Rock where she could be close to him. She had been less than receptive about it the last time they'd talked, but this time he would insist. It would be difficult at first, but given her heart condition she would finally come to see the sense in it. By fall Lucas could quit worrying about his mother out on the lake, miles from town, rattling around in that big house all by herself.

CHAPTER ONE

JANET GALLEN FELT as if she had just followed Alice through the looking glass. And landed right in the middle of the White Rabbit's tea party. The woman bustling around the cluttered kitchen bore no physical resemblance to Alice's rabbit, but there was little doubt they were kindred spirits. An overage, overweight beagle eyed her nervously from a rocking chair.

The kitchen of the farmhouse was a strange mixture of old and new, with a huge Home Comfort wood cook stove presiding over a new gas range and an ancient dishwasher. A small microwave oven sat on top of a lovely oak pie safe. Yellowed, curling recipes, snipped long ago from newspapers were tacked here and there. Stoneware, cast-ironware and baskets sat and hung everywhere, a collector's dream. As Janet scanned the crowded but cozy room, her eyes widened when they came to rest on a lump of something furry, which Janet took for a cat, lying sprawled in and around an old Dutch oven on a shelf above the stove, its tail flung over a fat, smiling cookie jar. She couldn't tell whether the cat was alive, dead or a stuffed toy and was a little afraid to ask. Janet waved the *Mother Earth News* at her hostess. "Mrs. McNair, about your ad?"

"My dear, you can't imagine how glad I am to see you. You're the first *normal* person to answer the ad. And a real RN. I had no idea how many strange people there were wandering around looking for a home."

"Mrs. McNair, perhaps you could tell me a little—"

"Call me Bea, dear. If you'll just let me get these dratted watercress sandwiches done. I don't suppose you know how to keep them from being soggy, do you?"

Janet had driven two hundred miles to answer the rather peculiar ad and had already concluded that whatever this job was, it wasn't what she had in mind for the Big Change in her life, but she couldn't help smiling at the woman struggling over the soggy tea sandwiches. "I think you need to dry the watercress."

"Oh, I tried that, but it looked so limp and dull."

"Maybe one of those whirly things for salad that centrifuge the water off." Janet stood up and examined one of the sandwiches. It seemed to consist of a lump of soggy Wonder bread smothered in wet watercress. She looked away, to keep from laughing, and into a slitted yellow eye above the stove. A whisker twitched and the eye closed. Janet waited for the cat to grin and disappear.

"Well, it's most distressing. I mean, how can one have a proper tea without watercress sandwiches?"

"A proper tea?" Alice and the White Rabbit floated across her mind's eye. "I don't suppose you have any white rabbits around," she murmured.

"Oh, how did you know? Poor little Lucas. But his rabbit was gray. Edgar's old bluetick hound took it for a wild one. Lucas has never forgiven him, which worries me a little with Edgar here. But Lucas will just have to forgive Edgar and his old hound. Anyway, I do think tea is such an important part of things. I'm trying them out on Verla and Edgar. Not that they would know a proper tea if they saw one—or remember it ten minutes later sometimes, but I just know you'll make them right as rain in no time. So there you are."

Janet wondered very much at that moment just where she was, what she was doing there and, more to the point, what Bea was talking about. The ad had mentioned a business enterprise and the need for a nurse, but darned if Janet could see any business—unless it had to do with catering high teas, and that seemed unlikely given the isolated setting on a lake in northern Arkansas. And the condition of the watercress sandwiches. "Maybe if you used butter instead of mayonnaise."

The older woman clapped her hands. "Of course. It wouldn't soak through. My, that's such a load off my mind. Oh dear, I've neglected you so. Well, now, would you like tea or coffee?"

Janet hated hot tea, but she was afraid a request for coffee might start another flurry of activity. "Tea's fine." She watched as Beatrice McNair set out an old china tea set and an obscenely rich coffee cake. And no watercress sandwiches. Janet judged the woman to be in her late sixties or early seventies. She was short and round, with pure white hair and bright blue eyes that twinkled a good deal. She had good eyes, but then Janet supposed the same might have been said of Alice, particularly after she got to Wonderland. Janet sneaked a quick look toward the stove to see if the cat was still there. The yellow eye winked at her and the whiskers twitched. She smiled nervously as Bea finally sat down and poured tea.

"I'm going to turn this place into a bed and breakfast establishment."

Janet almost choked on her coffee cake.

"You see, it all started with Verla and Edgar. I whisked Verla out of that dreadful nursing home last week, and she's only now beginning to know who I am. And poor Edgar can't even get in one. So, I naturally thought a few paying guests would make it all possible. But, of course, with Edgar, I really do need a nurse until we know if it's permanent. And then, well, Lucas couldn't possibly expect me to abandon my new business for the shuffleboard courts."

The old lady beamed, and Janet's head reeled as she tried to make sense of the conversation. "Your children don't know about this?"

"Heavens no. Lucas will be slightly annoyed, but he'll come around. Jessica ... well, she tends toward hysteria in all things. But she lives in Tulsa and never comes home, anyway."

"But—"

"You see, I had a heart attack three years ago." She leaned close to demonstrate with thumb and forefinger how small the attack had been. "A very tiny attack, but I still have some angina, and Lucas is just beside himself. Oh, dear, I'm making a mess of the whole thing. Let me start from the beginning...."

A FEW WEEKS LATER, Janet threw open the door of the rambling house to let in the spring breeze and sunshine, taking a moment to look out across the lake and inhale deeply of the fresh Ozark air. The house sat perched on the edge of the lake as if it had been planned, but in fact it had originally overlooked the river valley, long before the government had even thought of damming up the river. All that water had made her nervous at first, revived her bad feelings about water, but she'd grown used to it. After all, she didn't have to get *in* it, and it was lovely. The redbuds were just beginning to show pink, and the dogwoods would follow hard on their heels, painting the hillsides with delicate colors. It was a drastic change from her small apartment near the hospital in Little Rock, but in one short month she'd fallen in love with the place and couldn't imagine ever going back to the city.

She'd never worked so hard in all her life, but she and Bea McNair had turned the old farmhouse into a charming bed and breakfast establishment in record time. Well, mostly a bed and breakfast place. Edgar and Verla were firmly ensconced in rooms on the second floor.

After the initial interview, Janet knew that Bea's idea was absolutely crazy, and she'd had serious questions about the sanity of the woman herself. But the more she thought about it—every time she went to work, every time she saw some doctor or resident who reminded her of Jack—and the more she began to drag around and think like a Victorian governess in a gothic novel, the more appealing the idea sounded. If it didn't pan out, she could always go back to a hospital. Janet thought of it as a working vacation, but deep down, she *knew* it was going to succeed. They would *make* it work—if she could keep Bea on track. Bea was determined to keep her house and take care of her friends, all of which deeply touched Janet. Bea insisted her angina was better than it had been in months, and Janet had seen the sparkle that comes of being needed grow daily in Bea's eyes.

Janet smoothed her cotton dress and stopped for a quick glance in the hall mirror. She wasn't much of a mirror gazer—more of a glancer and preferably at mirrors that hung high on the wall. She had what people kindly referred to as a classic figure, a term which Janet interpreted to mean broad across the beam, unless you were Venus or one of her crew. But today Janet didn't care. She didn't even care that the sunshine had brought out more freckles and bleached her short, sandy-red hair a lighter shade. She felt good. It even occurred to her that she looked like an advertisement for milk, all rosy and freckled and windblown. She posed before the mirror, an imaginary glass of milk held to her cheek. Well, milkmaid beat gothic heroine any day of the week.

Their first real guests were due today, and she was bubbling over with nervous energy and excitement. Bea was in the kitchen getting ready for afternoon tea. A lifelong admirer of Agatha Christie, Bea had carried on with her plans for afternoon tea in the finest tradition of Miss Marple. The watercress sandwiches were actually showing promise, and Bea was hinting at the possibility of a murder weekend, just like they had at bigger inns in Eureka Springs and Memphis. After much discussion and a few threats Janet had even convinced Bea that Clarence the cat and his Dutch oven had to be moved to the floor behind the stove—just in case a health inspector dropped by. She had the distinct impression that Clarence had not forgiven her. Now if she could just convince Bea that Inez was not going to be much of a maid until after the baby was born....

Janet wandered into the front parlor, which now served as a sitting room and reception area. Verla Smallwood sat in an overstuffed chair knitting an afghan which deserved a place in *The Guinness Book of Records* as the World's Largest Afghan, if she ever finished it. Janet had asked Bea about the creation, but Bea assured her Verla had never been able to crochet worth a toot. Verla, in her eighties, arthritic and a little forgetful, had landed in a nursing home when she refused to sell the four-room house she'd lived in for fifty years. Her children had "thought it best." She had come out of the nursing home *more* than a little forgetful, Janet thought angrily, looking at the woman. A very pregnant teenager sat beside her, trying to crochet a baby blanket that looked suspiciously like the afghan in design and size. The girl looked as if she'd been pregnant for years.

Verla looked up and smiled. "When are we going to eat?"

"Well, since we just finished lunch, Verla, it may be a little while. Afternoon tea is at four and that's three hours away." She knelt beside the old woman and admired her knitting.

Inez rolled her baby blanket into a ball and laid it aside. "Of course she remembers lunch, don't you Verla? Remember how much you liked those sweet potatoes? Just like you used to grow, you said." She looked up at Janet. "She was doing real well this morning but some afternoons she kinda forgets things. I'll just go get her a little snack to tide her over." The girl managed to get to her feet with a great deal of groaning and lumbered off to the kitchen.

"Fine." Janet marveled at how good Inez was with Verla and how perfectly hopeless the girl was in the kitchen. The kitchen seemed to evoke endless crying jags and groaning, all of which drove Janet crazy. Janet had almost decided that Inez had been traumatized by a cook stove in her childhood. It was the only thing to explain her radical behavior.

"Did we really just have lunch?" Verla asked doubtfully.

"Sure did, but Inez is fixing you a little something." With much face crinkling, Verla finally remembered. Janet patted her on the arm and stood up. When she turned around, she saw a man standing in the doorway, silently watching.

Janet stood staring for a long moment, her hand on the back of Verla's chair for support. He was tall, with chestnut brown hair and eyes the color of fine dark chocolate. Mid-thirties, she thought, with high cheekbones and ruggedly chiseled, well-tanned features. White Levi's and a striped polo shirt clung to his body like a second skin. He stood feet spread, one hand on the door facing, the other on his hip, looking for all the world like a cover of *Yachting for Hunks* come to life. Janet still stared, and wondered what she should do, forgetting for the moment that he might be a guest and belong there. He had the kind of eyes—not to mention body—that inspired loss of memory.

She finally got herself moving toward him. Nothing like a hostess who stands and stares like a dimwit, she thought. Then she realized he must be Pete Bradley, the artist they were expecting, yet... Janet mentally shook herself and took a few more tentative steps. She forced her most dazzling smile and attributed her nervousness to "first guest" jitters. "Mr. Bradley?"

"Who are you?" He appeared to be confused, and stared at her as if she were a specimen from some other planet.

Janet felt her face flush under the close scrutiny as she looked up into his dark eyes. "I'm Janet Gallen. We weren't expecting you quite this early. If you'd just sign our register." She felt her control return...mostly. Of course, her face was burning up and her heart seemed to be running away with itself, but other than that...

Janet felt his eyes settle on her red face—eyes that belonged to Heathcliffe and dark, brooding moors. *Oh, no, she was doing her Victorian governess thing again.* She turned the register toward him, lecturing herself sternly that this was Beaver Lake, not some dank tarn, but somehow one didn't expect bed and breakfast guests to look like brooding, gothic hunks.

He stared at the register with Crow's Rest Bed and Breakfast Inn neatly stenciled across the top. "What, may I ask, is going on here?" His features creased into a frown—a serious frown. A *really* serious frown. His eyes questioned her intently.

Janet looked at the register—upside down—searching for the source of his irritation, but she saw no misprints or obvious irregularities. She looked up, into chocolaty eyes now flashing almost black. "I beg your pardon? We ask all our guests to sign the register." She pushed the register closer to him and smiled, trying to ignore the heavy scent of male emanating from him. She was used to men in hospital greens who smelled of alcohol and biodine.

When he finally grabbed the register and scrawled his name, paying little attention to the lines, she sighed in relief, thinking he was carrying the temperamental artist thing a little far. He shoved it back to her and she read the name. Lucas McNair. Her heart seemed to pop up into her throat. Lucas McNair, as in "poor little Lucas" with the gray bunny. Bea's son. Bea's son who wanted her to move to Little Rock. Bea's son who "might be a little annoyed, but will come around." Her head snapped up, her eyes wide as she stared at him. She tried to smile confidently. Bea had shown her fuzzy snapshots of her son, but they bore little resemblance to the son in the flesh. Janet stared back at the register, then up again at the man and considered the logistics of squirming her classic figure into the woodwork. She tried to explain. "Oh. I thought . . . I mean we were expecting . . . well, we, uh . . ."

He leaned close, his voice velvet on steel. "I repeat my question. What the hell is going on here?"

Janet felt her pulse rate soar to Boston Marathon level, whether from the appearance of the problem son or from his closeness she wasn't sure. "Uh, I guess Bea didn't have time to tell you, did she?" She tried another dazzling smile, which didn't quite come off.

"Tell me what?" He stepped around the desk, trapping her.

At that moment, Verla got up and hobbled toward them, struggling to bring her afghan along. She pointed an accusing finger at Lucas. "I know you. You're—" Her face crinkled in thought. "Anyway, I know you, and I hope you'll get this place straightened out. A body could starve here." She started toward the stairs, king-size afghan trailing behind. Suddenly she turned and pointed a gnarled finger. "You're little Lukie." She winked at Janet. "See? Didn't think I knew, did you?" With that she started up the stairs.

Janet tried to laugh, hoping he would see the humor in the situation—actually hoping he would see anything but her. "Verla is a little forgetful sometimes. But she's getting better every day." She waved toward the stairs. "Medication. Temporary. Nursing home." Since she wasn't even making sense to herself, she shut up.

"Verla Smallwood? What in the hell is she doing here?" His frown turned to a look of confusion again.

During his momentary puzzlement, Janet's crisis training finally surfaced, and she pushed all thoughts of Heathcliffe and moors aside. It was time to take control of the situation—or at least pass the buck and the hunk to Bea. "Your mother is in the kitchen. I'm sure she has a lot to tell you." She started down the hall, conscious of his gaze burning into her backside. To distract him she tossed her head, a gesture totally inappropriate for short curly hair, she realized too late. All it did was make her dizzy. He probably thought she was having a seizure. And maybe she was.

She steamed toward the kitchen, anxious to turn him over to Bea and be about her work. Or at least get away from those eyes and that look of befuddlement, which was going to turn into anger at any minute. "Bea, guess who's here?" she announced brightly as they reached the kitchen door.

Bea was busy rolling out dough and explaining the art of scone making to Inez, who sat in a chair groaning and holding her belly. Janet started to suggest she go back to Verla and the jumbo afghans, then thought better of it. "Forget the snack, Inez. Verla went to her room."

The fat beagle leaped from his rocking chair in the corner and flung himself at Lucas, all waggling and whining. Lucas bent to ruffle the dog's fur. "Hi, Scooter. How's my boy?" The dog's tail wig-wagged for a moment, then Scooter raced back to his chair to watch Lucas closely. Clarence twitched a whisker and refused to be drawn into the homecoming. Lucas "fuzzled" him anyway.

Bea wiped a flour-laden hand at her permed hair and looked up. Bea might have to call the sheriff for a ride during icy spells, Janet thought, but she never missed her weekly appointment at Fran's Beauty

Shop. A smile broke over her wrinkled face, and her eyes twinkled. "Lucas, dear. What a wonderful surprise. Why didn't you call?" She wiped her hands on her apron and held them out to her son. "Poor Scooter doesn't hear like he used to. See, he's embarrassed because he didn't hear you." She glanced at the dog, nestled in its chair, tail wagging furiously. "Clarence is a little out of sorts—Janet moved him— but we can't have cat hair drifting into the guests' soup, can we?" she whispered.

Janet groaned.

Lucas hugged his mother and dropped a kiss on her forehead. "I thought I would surprise you, but it seems I'm the one to be surprised." The frown melted away when he kissed her. "Mother, perhaps we could have a little talk?" The frown returned as he glanced at Janet and Inez.

"Certainly, dear. Just as soon as I get the scones on to bake." Bea rolled the dough with new vigor.

"Scones?" His withering look toward Janet clearly indicated this entire situation was all her fault.

"Of course, dear. Oh, I had so hoped to surprise you. I was going to make pineapple upside down cake when you came."

Lucas laughed, but the sound had a certain strained quality to it. "Well, you certainly did surprise me all right. Would you like to tell me just what is going on here?" He leaned against the counter, arms across his chest.

Bea beamed. "Janet and I have opened a bed and breakfast place. And we've taken Edgar in, although we're not at all sure of his prognosis, and we're helping Verla after her dreadful experience at the nursing home. And we have room for at least three more. Isn't it wonderful?'' she said breathlessly.

"Edgar Guinn?'' he asked incredulously.

"Of course, you remember Edgar. Now you must be nice to Edgar. After all, it wasn't his fault that dog of his got your rabbit. I tried to tell you a gray rabbit was a mistake, but you didn't like the white ones. You thought their pink eyes were funny. Anyway, Janet was a godsend. I couldn't have managed otherwise.''

Lucas turned back to Janet, eyes flashing. "I'll just bet. Was this all her idea?''

With the firm intention of blending into the wallpaper, Janet tried to slip out into the hall, but a strong hand snaked out and stopped her. Warmth rushed up her arm as he hauled his quarry back to stand beside him.

Bea chattered on. "Of course it wasn't, Lucas, but I simply couldn't have done it without her.''

"I'll just bet.'' He pulled Janet close to him, his lips uncomfortably close to her ear. "I don't know what this is all about, but I intend to find out. She would *never* have done something like this on her own.''

Janet's temper flared in spite of his closeness—or, she was afraid, because of it. "If you understood your mother's feelings about her home and friends, you'd know very well she would. Anything would be better than moving to Little Rock and becoming part of the shuffleboard set.'' With that, she pulled away, straightened to her full five foot four and stalked to the front of the house, face red, hair bobbing.

Lucas slammed a fist against the door jamb, all semblance of restraint gone. "I don't know what you're doing, Mother, but whatever it is, you should have consulted me." Scooter buried his head. Inez groaned and Lucas seemed to really notice her for the first time. "And who is this?"

Bea deftly cut the dough, ignoring her son's outburst. "You see, Inez, you just use the biscuit cutter. It's as easy as can be." The girl heaved herself up and carefully cut out a scone, groaning throughout the procedure, then returned to her chair. Bea smiled proudly at her son. "This is Inez. She's our maid."

Inez waved a limp hand at Lucas. "Hi."

It was Lucas's turn to groan. "Only my mother would hire a maid, then do all the work herself."

Bea leaned across the table and whispered loudly. "Well, she's pregnant, dear."

Lucas cast a dubious look at Inez. "I'm glad you told me, Mother. I never would have known." He turned to leave.

"Well, she's the only one who can do a thing with Verla, although I really must help her with her blanket. Verla does not do fine work at all well. I'm afraid she'll ruin Inez for good. But Inez is not used to kitchens. We're working on that."

Lucas sighed. "Mother, I'm not about to ask you what you're talking about. I'm going to take a long walk and cool off, then we are going to have a serious talk. A very serious talk." He stalked out of the kitchen before she could produce any more surprises. Scooter hit the floor and raced after him.

Bea hurried after him, rolling pin in hand. "Oh, Lucas dear, if you're planning to stay, you'll have to take one of the attic rooms. Everything else is booked up with guests. Oh, and don't forget tea at four."

Janet buried her head in the register, peering out of the corner of her eye as Lucas McNair strode past her, looking for all the world like an angry Greek god come off his mountain to hand out wrath and retribution to his errant mortals. She wiped her brow, pushed wisps of hair back in place and thought it was going to be a very long weekend, all the while trying to ignore the strange feelings coursing through her mind and body. The kind of feelings she'd always thought might occur if Harrison Ford were to appear at her door one day to whisk her away to exotic places. This wasn't Harrison Ford, but if there was any whisking to be done, she had a sinking feeling she might just be the whiskee. She considered disappearing for a long trip to the grocery—maybe the whole weekend.

As she peeked through the curtains and watched him walk toward the boat dock, Scooter trundling along at his heels, she wondered if she should follow and try to explain, but somehow she didn't think he was interested in her explanations. Of course, that was really Bea's department but, then, Bea's explanations were not always as illuminating as they might be.

She sighed. What in the world was she going to do? He seemed the sort of man who got what he wanted— and if he wanted Bea in Shuffleboard City, he wouldn't stop until he got her there.

Janet tapped the counter, her anger growing by the minute. "Over my dead body, Mr. Lucas McNair," she muttered, waving a fist in his general direction.

CHAPTER TWO

JANET HURRIED toward the kitchen when she saw Lucas turn and look at the house. The smile on his face worried her. It certainly made him all the more striking, but somehow she got the impression that it was not a smile of happiness. It was the kind of smile that spoke of something else—plans, strategies... whisking!

Clarence had abandoned his Dutch oven for the kitchen table where he bathed a paw in slow motion. A freshly baked scone lay beside him, half-eaten. Janet fussed at him and he turned his smug, crumb-laden face in her direction, then continued his bathing. She felt her composure begin to slip and had to bite her tongue to keep from lashing out at Inez, who sat watching Clarence and groaning. "Bea, Inez, we simply can't have Clarence on the table sampling the scones. The health department man would not be amused," she said as brightly as she could manage.

Bea swooped Clarence and his scone off the table and lectured him severely. "He just doesn't realize about rules and guests and things, dear. But I'll have a long talk with him tonight."

Janet smiled through clenched teeth, ignoring Clarence's Cheshire cat look, wishing he'd do the disappearing act instead of just grinning. She loved Bea dearly, but there were times—"Well, I'm sure he doesn't, but we must be firm." She turned to Inez. "Since you want something else to do, Inez, why don't we put you in charge of Clarence. You can keep him off things. Okay?" She spoke more sharply than she'd intended and regretted it immediately, but much as she hated to admit it, Bea's son had her more than a little flustered.

Inez burst into tears. "I'll leave. I'm just a burden," she sobbed.

Janet sighed and gave serious consideration to flogging Inez with a scone. Instead, she knelt in front of the girl and took her hand. "You're fine. All you have to do is keep Clarence off the stove and table," she said gently.

"But my baby will look like a cat if I touch him." Her sobs got louder.

Janet rocked back on her heels, incredulity written on her face. Inez was basically a good kid, and was good with Verla and Edgar, but Janet had discovered in the past few weeks that Inez had an almost infinite capacity to drive sane people right up the wall. She knew it was all related to the pregnancy and the girl's fears, but sometimes, Janet's Irish temper got overloaded. "Oh, for crying out loud, that's the silliest thing I ever heard," Janet muttered, her patience gone.

"It's an old wives' tale, dear. Inez, it really is nonsense." Bea bent over the oven and peered in.

Inez sobbed louder, and Janet chewed a knuckle to keep from shaking the girl. She got up and retreated to the table.

Bea slapped a pan of fresh scones on the table and whispered in Janet's ear. "It'll all work out, dear." She winked and bustled out of the room on some errand.

"Right." Janet felt hot and out of sorts as she busied herself with hot scones and boiling water and wondered about her sanity. It was too early for tea, but with Edgar and Verla it never seemed to matter. She walked around the groaning Inez, wishing for the umpteenth time that Bea had not hired Inez as the maid—at least until the baby was born. "I'm sorry I fussed at you, Inez. I'm just nervous about the guests and all. Why don't you go lie down?" she asked, determined to regain her composure in the face of the bedlam.

"It's worse when I lay down. Besides, I oughta do something useful."

"Hey, it's all right. We'll work you twice as hard after the baby comes. Just watch the cat, okay? I guarantee you it will have no effect on the baby. Absolutely guarantee it." The girl's lower lip quivered, but she nodded. "Thank you, Inez. That's a great load off my mind." Almost unconsciously, Janet noted the girl's color and the amount of swelling in her legs. She's got enough problems, she thought. Inez was the granddaughter of a dear friend of Bea's. Her mother had demanded she give the baby up, then kicked her out when Inez refused. Now good old Mom was making noises about forcing an adoption. And the baby's father—he'd refused to marry Inez—was suddenly making noises about custody. Maybe Janet could distract Lucas with the girl's legal problems. Let him deal with mothers who told their pregnant daughters dreadful things. That should keep his level of confusion at an acceptable level.

Bea bustled back into the kitchen, her face flushed. "Edgar was determined to go look for his train. I had quite a time convincing him it was late today. He does so love to dream about his train days. I know you said we should humor him, but I feel so silly rushing about looking for trains."

Janet smiled. Poor Edgar. They were basically taking care of him until he could qualify for financial help. He was another body fallen through the government safety net. "I know it sounds crazy, Bea, but jerking him back to the present upsets him terribly and embarrasses him. The less stress, the more lucidity. Anyway that's my theory. He's been through a lot and he's staying in the present a little more each day, so I think we're on the right track." She slid scones onto a china plate. "I think everything's ready, Bea." She wanted to get tea with the hunk over with and go to her room, maybe have a quiet nervous breakdown.

"Well, it is early, but Lucas is no doubt starved from his drive." She looked up just as her son walked through the door. A breathless Scooter thundered toward the kitchen and his rocking chair and the bit of warm, buttery scone Bea had saved for him. "Oh, there you are. Haven't we done a lovely job, dear?"

Lucas hugged his mother and planted a noisy kiss on her cheek. "You certainly have. It was quite a shock, I can tell you." He looked from his mother to Janet. "What's with all the red faces? Do I detect a note of frazzle here?"

Bea fussed with the teapot. "Inez is a little upset dear. About Clarence and her baby."

"What does Clarence have to do with her baby?"

Inez burst out in fresh sobs. Janet made a strange noise. "Bea, let's not get into all this again. Let's just have tea. I'm sure Mr. McNair is famished." She smiled sweetly, jaws clenched tight.

He lounged against the wall. "Oh, I would love to hear about it—whatever it is."

Bea set the teapot on the tray. "Inez is very sensitive right now, dear. Have you had a chance to see what we've done?"

"Not yet. I'm still in shock. Perhaps Janet can give me a guided tour later." He grinned at her and reached to brush a spot of flour off her nose.

Bea sighed and fluffed her hair. "Well, I would have told you, but I knew you would try to talk me out of it. Be honest, now. You would have."

"I would have." He looked straight into Janet's eyes. "Of course, I would never have thought you could find such competent help."

"Oh, Janet is just wonderful. I simply couldn't manage without her."

"I'm sure." He smiled that smile again as his gaze trailed down her body, then came back to rest on her face.

Janet felt her already-flushed face redden another shade under his careful scrutiny. The message was loud and clear. She knew this sudden smiling, butter-wouldn't-melt man was more dangerous than the frowning one. Lucas McNair had figured out some way to put the skids to their bed and breakfast operation and perhaps get rid of her in the process. Then he could whisk Bea away to Shuffleboard City. Well, Mr. Lucas McNair would find out that Janet Gallen didn't abandon people quite that easily. She was committed to Bea's enterprise, and she would see it through. Just as soon as her heart stopped pounding. "Bea is the one who thought of the plan. I just helped her a little." She refused to admit anything to this man with the chocolaty eyes, eyes that seemed to look right into her soul—not to mention right through her clothes.

She gathered up the tea tray, rather gracefully she thought considering her state of frazzle, and headed for the dining room, determined to remain calm and cool in the face of what she was sure, sooner or later, would turn into a family free-for-all. He was a stubborn headstrong man, but beneath it, Janet sensed... something else. Better she concentrate on "stubborn." The "something else" was probably all her imagination, she told herself as she stumbled on the edge of a throw rug and almost upended the tea tray.

Lucas carried the scones, one arm still around his mother's shoulders. "Well, you ladies must tell me everything you're doing. It's fascinating. Perhaps I can help you with the legal end."

Bea laughed. "Legal end? Lucas, dear, we're not running the Hilton. We're just running a tiny business."

"Ah, but there are still legal ramifications, Mother."

Janet set the tea things down and flashed a smile in Lucas's general direction, carefully avoiding his eyes. "I think, Mr. McNair, that you will find we have taken care of all the required permits and such." She knew what he was trying to do. The old scare tactic routine—scare them into abandoning their project with talk of liability and such. She set out tea cups with an unsteady hand, wishing he'd stop staring at her.

He smiled back. "Oh? Are you licensed by the state to operate a nursing home?"

Bea poured tea. "Oh, Lucas, you do have such a legal mind." She turned to Janet. "He always was a worrier and a stickler for detail. That's why he's such a good lawyer." She handed Lucas his cup. "We're not running a nursing home, dear. I had Mr. Twimbly draw up the papers. We sold Verla and Edgar their rooms. Just like a condominium. Everyone's buying condos on the lake these days." Her eyes danced.

Lucas made choking sounds, and Janet watched his neck turn red. She felt the explosion coming, but at least Bea's announcement had wiped that smug grin off his handsome face. She took great consolation in that.

"You did what?" he croaked.

Bea offered her son a scone. "Crow's Rest Condos. It has a nice ring, doesn't it?"

Lucas took a deep breath, and a muscle twitched in his jaw. "Mother, you know old man Twimbly hasn't read a law book in fifty years. It can't be legal." His voice was tightly controlled.

"Of course it is, dear. Janet looked into it."

"Oh? Are you an attorney, Janet?"

Lucas was ready to blow up. Janet fully expected her dress to catch on fire any minute from those flashing eyes. Not that she would feel it. Maybe she should take shelter in Clarence's Dutch oven until the worst was over. She quickly cast that idea aside. Clarence wasn't the type to share. "No, but it's perfectly legal. When they die, their interest reverts to your mother. Since they own their residences, or are considered owners, they are not denied any social services benefits, which they would be denied if they didn't have their own place." Janet wondered how such a calm voice could come out of such a nervous wreck.

She forced a smile and told her rising temper to cool it. "But, then, I'm sure you know all about red tape and loopholes like that, don't you?" Let him put that in his pipe and smoke it. Janet might not be a lawyer, but she'd worked in hospitals long enough to know how old folks could be shafted by the system. And she'd learned a few things about helping them.

Lucas set his cup down with a clatter and reached for Janet's arm. "Mother, will you excuse us please? It seems that Janet and I have some legal matters to discuss."

Bea frowned. "But you haven't had a scone." She smiled as Lucas bent over and scooped up two scones. "Janet, would you call Edgar and Verla for tea on your way out? Inez can't seem to manage the stairs."

Janet was able to stop their forward progress long enough to call up the stairs, then found herself being dragged out the door and toward the boat dock. She wondered if he planned to drown her. As she stumbled along after him, she decided that perhaps a good dunking would be just the thing. She would have cardiac arrest the minute she hit the water and that would solve the problem. And put out the fire running up her arm and radiating throughout her body. She jogged along, trying to keep up with his long strides.

"Sit," he ordered when they reached the wooden benches on the rickety boat dock, handing her a slightly worse-for-wear scone.

Janet sat, trying to ignore the sound of the lake lapping about right under her feet, the boats wallowing nearby and the familiar fear rising within her. She'd never ventured onto the dock or into the faded boat house. Too close to the water. The old tension rose and mingled with all the new tension and she squelched an urge to run. How in the world had she managed to get herself into this mess? Why couldn't Bea's son be short and ugly and sell used cars and not care what his mother did with the family home?

"Now. Do you have any idea at all of the liability situation in which you have put my mother?" He paced the dock like a tiger—a mad tiger.

"*I* have not put your mother into any situation. I have helped her do what she wants to do." Suddenly, Janet's temper—or her fear of falling over backward into the water—began to take charge. "If you hadn't scared her to death threatening to drag her off to a retirement home, she never would have done it."

Lucas turned to stare at her, incredulity written on his face. "Threaten? I've never threatened anyone in

my life. I just talked with her about the possibilities."
He gestured at her with the scone between bites.

"You talked *at* her. She wasn't participating." She
watched his whole body tense and knew she was getting in over her head, but something about him
brought out her temper, a temper best kept under
control.

"I don't believe this. She didn't agree or disagree."

"I rest my case," Janet said smugly, concentrating
on the water lapping at the shore instead of that magnificent body. Both views made her stomach roll. She
decided to plunge ahead. Maybe she could make him
so mad he'd just leave. "Why are you so mad? Why
can't you just accept it and be happy for your
mother?"

"Accept it? You've got to be kidding. I don't know
how you did it, but somehow you managed to get my
mother into a situation that I may or may not be able
to get her out of." He turned and stared at her, fists
clenched on his hips.

Janet stood up and glared at him. "Then why don't
you just go back to Little Rock and leave her alone.
She's doing what she wants to do. She's staying in her
own home, she's making a little extra money, and she's
helping her neighbors and people she cares about.
She's no longer lonely or alone." Janet's heart
pounded as she pleaded her case—and it wasn't all
from anger.

"She's supposed to be making plans to move to a
retirement home in Little Rock, not starting a board-
ing house for senile neighbors at age sixty-eight. Chil-

dren rebel. Mothers don't. That's...some kind of rule.''

"She doesn't want to go to a retirement home. Even *I* know that." She didn't doubt that Lucas really wanted what was best for his mother, but his idea of best and Bea's idea of best were poles apart. Janet had to make him understand that—so he would go away.

Lucas turned, stalked toward her and stopped, his face inches from hers. "She *thinks* she doesn't. When she gets there, she'll love it. I'm sure of it. I've done a lot of research on this, you know."

"I'm sure you have—with other offspring who are convinced their parents will love whatever it is they've planned for them. But your mother won't. She'll hate it. And what about Scooter? And Clarence—although I'm sure he could pass for an art deco knick-knack." Janet's head spun with the smells of after-shave and angry male. She could see a vein pounding in his neck.

Lucas chose to ignore the dog issue. "I've known my mother longer than you have. How did you get to be such an authority on what she loves and hates?" He towered over her, eyes flashing.

"Because I don't go around with my mind made up in advance. That's how. Everybody thinks they know what's best for old people, but they never bother to ask them what *they* want." Janet turned away from him, unable to think with him looming so close. She knew her face was bright red by now.

He sat down on a bench and looked at her, something new in his eyes. "Well, how the hell did she get from wanting to stay in her own home to running a combination bed and breakfast, nursing home condo, or whatever you call it? Are you going to tell me she thought that up all by herself?'' Some of the anger seemed to be gone from his voice, replaced by incredulity. He absentmindedly took a bite of his scone.

Janet breathed a sigh of relief and nervously nibbled at her scone, hoping it might quell the rolling in her stomach. Perhaps after the initial shock, he was going to accept what his mother had done. "It's a long story, but actually, she did. It started with Verla and Edgar. Edgar has had a light stroke and has no place to go. Not to mention no income. Verla's family had moved her to a local nursing home. Bea just couldn't stand seeing Verla waste away a little more each time she went to visit.''

Janet warmed to her subject, suddenly anxious to make this man understand what Bea had done and why. "Bea obviously couldn't afford to just take them in, so she figured she could take a little bit of money from them—they don't have much, you know—then take in paying guests for profit, and it would all work out.'' Janet looked straight into Lucas's eyes, trying to ignore the fact that they reminded her of some dark, mysterious forest...and some other things. The flashing anger had turned to that something else— which Janet also chose to ignore. "Mr. McNair, your mother is an extraordinary woman.''

"Call me Lucas. You might as well, since we seem to be sharing the house for the next month.''

"Month?'' She almost choked on her scone. Her stomach danced and fluttered. This hunk—correction, mad hunk—would be sleeping just on the other side of a very thin wall from her for a month? Janet heaved a sigh of desperation.

"Month. In which time I have to figure out some way to convince my mother she's got a tiger by the tail." He got up, walked to the other side of the dock and leaned against the railing.

"Lucas, she's very happy doing this. Your approval would make her even happier." Did she detect a lessening of tension and anger? She was glad somebody's tension was lessening. Hers was growing by the minute.

"She's happy because she hasn't really done it yet. Look, I agree it's a wonderful idea—for someone else. She's a great lady, but that still doesn't change the fact that she has no business starting an operation like this. She needs to be with people her own age, in a secure environment. Close to me, close to good medical facilities." He stopped her objections with a hand. "Besides, what do either one of you know about running a bed and breakfast place? And how did *you* get involved in it?"

Janet flashed him a tremulous smile and waved her mangled scone in his direction. "Your mother put an ad in *Mother Earth News*."

Lucas shook his head and grinned. "You're kidding. I had no idea she even knew *Mother Earth News* existed. She really thought it up all by herself," he murmured. "Do you have experience in geriatrics? Or bed and breakfast?"

That quirky grin transformed his whole face, and Janet saw that little something she'd sensed before. Something she didn't want to see in him—a tenderness, a sensitivity, all those things she found so appealing in a man. "Not really. I'm just a nurse who was tired of the city life, needed a change. As for this business, what's to know? Guests get a bed at night and a muffin and orange juice for breakfast. And high tea in the afternoon. Maybe a murder on the weekend."

"Murder? Oh, God, what are you talking about now?"

"Miss Marple. Agatha Christie. Your mother reads mysteries." Surely he knew what his mother read. "She likes the idea of mystery weekends. You've heard of murder weekends."

He obviously didn't care to follow that line of discussion. "A clean bed. Are you telling me Inez is going to do all the hard work?"

"Not exactly. Inez may not have been one of your mother's better ideas. But she feels sorry for Inez. The girl has no place to go. I think most of her problem right now stems from the fact that she's scared to death. I hope she'll be okay after the baby comes. She shows a real knack for geriatrics when she's not hysterical. Verla will do anything for Inez, which is more than any of the rest of us can say."

Lucas laughed. "Verla... how I remember her. All us kids were scared to death of her because she was so fussy. We thought she was a witch."

Janet laughed and breathed easier. Lucas was clear across the dock from her and he'd quit staring and glaring. Now if he'd quit showing any signs of sensitivity, she'd be home free. Actually, at the moment, he was looking more than a little bewildered. Bewildered she could handle.

"I've heard of taking in stray dogs and cats, but stray people?" He shook his head and turned to gaze out over the lake.

"Inez will probably get another job as soon as the baby is born. Meanwhile she has no one to take care of her, a mother who's trying to take her to court and force her to give up the child at birth, and last but not least, she has the ability to drive me straight up the wall several times a day. Who knows, maybe you could help her." When she got no response, she shrugged. So much for that distraction.

"Look, she's a scared kid and she's having a rough time, but she does as much work as she can," Janet said quietly as she looked at Lucas's profile against the serene water and distant limestone bluffs. He was the kind of man women would die for. And Janet heard warning bells clanging in her head. Almost loud enough to drown out her pounding heart. She decided at that moment she'd best keep him mad and at arm's length if she was going to be sleeping next door to him, for a month. It would be hard to say no to a man like that if he pushed. Not that a man like him would push somebody like her, she thought. But thoughts of another handsome man made her cautious and tugged at the hurt she'd buried deep in her heart.

He turned back toward Janet and smiled. "My mother always was a softy for injured birds and dumped kittens, but there are programs to take care of people like Inez and Verla and Edgar. I might concede the possibility of her staying in her own home—might, I said." He paused, a rigid finger pointing at her. "I will never concede the possibility of her taking in every sad case that comes along. It's not her responsibility." He smiled again, not at Janet, but at some long lost memory of his mother perhaps. "I love her for it, but I won't let it kill her."

His smile almost took Janet's breath away. Lord, he was some kind of beautiful. "Lucas, you'll kill her if you take it away from her. I keep a very close eye on her health, you know. Her angina is stable, her blood pressure's good. She's going to give it her best shot, and so am I."

Lucas stared out over the lake and tapped his fingers against the railing for a long moment. When he finally turned toward her, he gave her a funny look. "And so am I." He started past her.

"What does that mean?" Suspicion bloomed. She'd thought for just a moment that he'd softened, but she knew now he would fight them all the way. And she had the sinking feeling he wouldn't fight fair.

Lucas touched the tip of his finger to the end of her nose. "Let's just let it be a surprise." He smiled. Dark eyes flashed mischievously.

A jolt of fire ran through her whole body as his finger slipped under her chin and tipped her head up, his lips close. This man was full of surprises, and at the moment none of them appealed to her. She backed away from the charged finger just in time to catch something new in his eyes. A question? A...oh, Lord, it was going to be a long month. "Well, I'd better go clean up after tea. Verla will be wanting supper soon.

I don't think she ate a bite the whole time she was in the nursing home. She's trying to make up.''

"You mean you're running a restaurant, too?"

"No. I don't think we could get Clarence past the health department. But we have to feed ourselves and the old folks." She stood up. "And you." She waved weakly, unsure how to end the conversation. "See you." She hurried past him, the hot spot on her nose totally unrelated to the warm day.

"Oh, you can count on seeing me again."

Janet didn't relish the idea of those eyes burning into her all the way to the house. She had seen the look when it changed from concern for his mother to something else. She almost ran, wondering how she was going to survive the month. But damned if he would run her off without a fight. She somehow had to make him understand how important this place was to Bea. Crow's Rest was where she'd borne and raised her children, where her husband had died. Where her lifetime and memories dwelled. Janet knew it was hard for children used to mobility to understand what a home meant to a woman, particularly an older woman. If she accomplished nothing else in the next month, she would have to make Lucas understand about roots. And make Bea and Inez understand about Clarence. And maybe drive herself crazy in the process.

CHAPTER THREE

JANET PUSHED the apple pie around on her plate. It had to be the first time in her life that she had no enthusiasm for apple pie, but she felt as if they had been at the dinner table for hours. Bea had beamed, Verla had eaten two of everything, an overexcited Edgar had rambled on about trains, Clarence had jumped up on Inez's lap, evoking a scream that would have done any slasher movie proud, and Lucas had stared—and eaten like a harvest hand. Janet felt the beginnings of a major revolt in her normally cast-iron stomach. Too much excitement, she kept telling herself.

She stood too quickly, almost upsetting her chair in the process, and started gathering dishes as if she were participating in the world's first dish-gathering race. Her only thought was to finish and get away from those staring, chocolaty eyes. He'd been hanging around all afternoon, shadowing her, watching her, knowing exactly the effect he caused. And since their first guest still hadn't shown, there was little for her to do but wander around. Between that and Inez calling her every time Clarence moved, she was near the end of her rope. Her only reprieve had come when he'd gone to shower and shave before dinner. In *her* attic bathroom.

Bea stood up. "Janet, dear, I'll take care of the dishes tonight. Why don't you take Lucas around and show him what all we've done?"

Janet piled dishes in the sink with a vengeance. She didn't want to take Mr. Yachting on tour. "I'll take care of them, Bea. You've done enough for today."

Suddenly Lucas was beside her. "I think that's a wonderful idea. Just leave the dishes. I'll help with them after the tour." He took Janet by the arm and led her into the hall.

Janet fumed silently as he steered her down the hall, trying to ignore her sudden warmth. She didn't know what he had in mind, but whatever it was, she didn't think she was going to like it. Or maybe she *would* like it, and that would be even worse. His clean, soapy smell wafted through her senses, mingling with his after-shave, which Janet was sure must be called Male. They stopped in the front foyer.

"Well?" He leaned against the wall and looked at her, a grin tugging at his mouth.

"Well what?" She looked down the hall, hoping for a distraction. Where was Edgar and his darn trains when you needed them?

"Where do we start the tour?"

His gaze trailed up and down her yellow voile sundress, and she longed to be wearing dirty jeans and a sloppy sweatshirt. "We don't. Surely you remember where everything is in this house." She couldn't imagine anything sillier than taking someone on a tour of a house in which they had grown up. Besides, she wasn't sure she could manage the stairs—she seemed to be rooted to the spot.

"But I want to see all these wonderful changes." His voice gently teased and prodded her.

"We did a lot of painting and we added one bathroom. In the attic." When she said it like that, it didn't sound like a lot of work. So why had she worked so darned hard for the last month? "And we refinished some furniture."

"And?" He rubbed his back against the wall.

Janet watched the muscles in his torso flex, and her stomach threatened revolt again. "A little wallpaper, a new dishwasher...actually, the house layout is perfect for this sort of thing."

"So show me." He nodded toward the stairs.

Janet shrugged and waved her hand toward the ceiling. "So what's a bed and breakfast? Beds and muffins. Let's skip the beds and I'll take you on a tour of the muffins in the morning." She tried to laugh, but all that came out was a series of small, strangled sounds. Perhaps she was going to have a heart attack. Which was ridiculous. She was a grown woman. A nurse. Used to men, used to flirting, used to a working atmosphere charged with sexual innuendo. *And look where it got you.*

His cheek twitched, and his voice sounded like dark, soft velvet. "I think I'd rather see the beds."

Janet felt rosy spots break out on her cheeks. The last thing she wanted to do was take Lucas McNair on a tour of the bedrooms. She strongly suspected he had in mind that old game, "entertain yourself with the hired help while you talk Mom into going away." She struggled to pull up her professional calm. Fortunately just then the door swung open and a slight young man with a great deal of hair entered, struggling under a weight of canvasses and other tools of an artist's trade. Janet scooted away from Lucas. She could have kissed the young man for showing up when he did. "*You* must be Mr. Bradley."

"Right," the young man murmured, blinking in the bright light of the hallway.

Janet grabbed his arm and practically dragged him to the desk. "If you would just sign the register, we'll get you settled in."

"Right. Great old place. Make great sketches." The young man struggled to follow Janet, strewing cases and canvasses in his trail.

"I'm sure it will." As Janet turned the register toward the young man, she wondered what kind of artist he was. Out of the corner of her eye, she saw Lucas shaking his head. She looked at the artist and gave him her most dazzling smile. He gave her a peculiar look and picked up the pen. As soon as Pete Bradley signed his name, Janet handed him a key and snatched up two of his cases. "If you'll just follow me."

Suddenly Lucas took the cases away from her and started up the stairs, pausing long enough to whisper in her ear. "You didn't know I used to be a bellhop, did you?"

Fuming again, Janet followed Lucas up the stairs and the artist followed her, answering "Right" to all her questions. She hurried to the front bedroom and opened the door. "North light, just as you requested. Bathroom's at the end of the hall. If we can do anything, just let us know." She smiled and raced out of the room, knowing it would be useless to converse further with a man whose vocabulary seemed to consist of "Right" and incomplete sentences. Maybe he was just tired—or weird. The way her luck was running, weird was more likely.

Lucas set down the cases with the rest of Pete's things and hurried out of the room to catch Janet. "While we're up here..."

"Oh, all right." She opened the door next to Pete's, flipped the light on, flipped it off and started to close the door. "That's it." But Lucas caught her arm, turned the lights back on, and ushered her into the lovely bedroom with its crisp spread and fresh flowers in tiny bud vases.

"Show me everything." He made a gesture with his hand to indicate the entire room. "Everything."

She went to the window, mostly to get away from him. He just wanted to play games, but Janet knew all too well that Lucas McNair was *not* the kind of man any woman in her right mind would play games with. "This is a window," she said mockingly. "From each guest room, we offer a lake view. As you can see, the rooms are furnished in basic Americana, a little Country Primitive, a little Late Salvation Army thrown in for good luck." She felt like a fool giving a tour of his own house. She walked to the door and started to turn, suddenly aware of his presence behind her. As she whirled around, Lucas was there, one hand on the door, the other against the old wardrobe—very neatly trapping her in the corner.

"What did you do with the pennants and the arrowheads?"

"Pennants and arrowheads?" Her mind reeled with his closeness and at his strange question. She sighed as realization dawned. Of all the rooms she could have picked, she would have to pick his old room.

He pointed toward the west wall. "St. Louis Cardinals all over that wall. I was going to pitch for them."

"You were?" Bea must have cleaned out his things before she arrived. She felt relieved when he turned away and walked to the middle of the room.

"And I had an extensive collection of arrowheads—pieces mostly—and rocks that only a vivid imagination could turn into an arrowhead. Every time Dad plowed, I followed him, searching for the perfect arrowhead. One that would slay the black panther I just knew lived on the other side of the river. If the arrowhead had a big chip out of it, I naturally figured it had been damaged when it hit a bear skull or some such. That way the chipped ones were just as important as the perfect ones. I wonder what Mom did with them."

Janet cleared her throat and imagined a little boy, poring over his collection. "Maybe the attic. I don't think she ever throws anything away."

"No, I don't think she does." He wandered around the room, touching things, seeing things that were no longer there.

"I take it this was your room?"

"Umm." He seemed to have forgotten Janet's presence. "I wonder if boys still look for Indian relics. Probably not. I guess most of them are at the bottom of the lake now."

Janet looked around the room, trying to see what he was seeing, trying to feel what he felt. They had papered the room, filled it with refinished furniture from the attic, swept away all the traces of a boy. "I'm sure it's all in the attic."

"What? Oh—I guess it doesn't matter." He shook his head and seemed to come back to the present. "Well, anything else of interest besides the view and the eclectic collection of furniture?" Before she could answer, he draped an arm over her shoulders and started toward the door. "You *have* done a nice job." She felt his fingers move over the smooth skin of her arm. "I want to see the rest."

"That's it. The rooms are similar—" she gasped, ducking out from under his arm before he felt her trembling. "I'm going to do the dishes now." She didn't want to hear any more reminiscences about boys following their father's plows and collecting arrowheads. It made him too... human, too... appealing.

"Yes, I suppose they are," he said distractedly. Lucas gave her a strange look and started down the stairs behind her. "I'll help with the dishes."

Janet growled aloud, her frustration and confusion growing by leaps and bounds. She needed to be alone, needed to think. "Don't bother. I can take care of them."

He smiled, looking totally in control again. "But I promised." He took the steps two at a time and was waiting in the kitchen when Janet got there.

"Why are you doing this?" There was no way she could handle Bea, Inez, Clarence, who was glaring at her from atop the stove, and Lucas all at the same time. She unwrapped Clarence from the cookie jar and deposited him behind the stove.

"Doing what?" he asked, the picture of innocence, bending to pet Scooter, whose tail wagged furiously.

"First you're ready to kill me and haul your mother away, now you're sweetness and light. What are you planning?" She started shoving dishes into the dishwasher.

"My, what a suspicious mind you have." He moved to the sink and handed her a rinsed plate.

When his fingers brushed hers, she jumped a bit but refused to look up. "You're plotting something. I can tell." She held the plate in midair.

"Maybe I'm just enjoying the scenery. Don't you advertise the finest scenery in the Ozarks?" His eyes wandered slowly over her body.

Janet rolled her eyes toward the ceiling, knowing full well he wasn't talking about lakes and trees. "Why me, Lord?" She turned to him, hands on her hips, face flushed. "Don't come on with the macho bit, okay? I know you want to force me to leave so Bea will go with you peaceably, but she's in full possession of her faculties, and as long as she wants to try this thing, I'm going to stick with her. So don't come on with the old seduction routine." She might as well head him off at the pass.

A frown creased his face as he studied her. "You really are committed to this crazy idea, aren't you?" When she just nodded instead of speaking, his frown grew. "Why? You're young, in your prime. Don't you want all the things a beautiful young woman would want?"

"And just what do you think that would be?" Now he wanted to play twenty questions. She could feel it coming. She began to shove dishes into the dishwasher with great abandon. "And don't call me beautiful. Okay?"

He stopped, a dish held in midair. "Oh, but you are."

Janet sighed, trying her best to ignore the desire flickering in his eyes. "Let's get back to twenty questions."

"Okay. You're a registered nurse. I know what Bea's paying you. And it doesn't track, Janet Gallen. You left a job in Little Rock that must have paid you in the twenty thousand dollar range to take one that pays practically nothing right now and may never pay much, and you're willing to fight to keep it. I have to ask myself why?"

Janet wasn't about to tell him why she'd left Little Rock, why she'd worked so hard for Bea. "Because I believe in what she's doing, that's why." She reached for a plate, but his hand caught her wrist. She felt her face flush.

"You don't really expect me to believe that, do you? Bea was a total stranger to you a month ago." His voice was silky, but the demand for answers was clear.

Janet stood her ground, in spite of her burning arm. They might as well get this straight right now. Then maybe he'd go away. "Your mother is an incredible lady."

"I know that. It still doesn't explain why you're here." His eyes bored into hers.

"That falls under the heading of *my* business," she snapped.

He pulled her closer, his hand clamped on her wrist. "Oh, I think it falls under the heading of my business, too, since it concerns my mother."

The impact of his words finally dawned on Janet. He must think she was trying to worm her way into Bea's good graces. Janet flushed. "If you think I'm trying to get money from Bea, then think again," she snapped, pulling away from him.

"Well, it is a thought. It happens." He calmly rinsed more dishes.

Janet sputtered and almost threw a plate on the floor. "How dare you even suggest such a thing!" Sparks flew between them as her eyes flashed deep blue.

"I'm not suggesting anything. I'm just trying to figure out what the hell you're doing here."

Janet had to admit the arrangement did sound strange, but she wasn't about to tell him the truth. Darn it, it wasn't any of his business. "I left Little Rock for personal reasons. And if that isn't good enough for you, then it'll just have to do." She busied herself with the dishes and controlling her temper, which was about to erupt.

"And do you not like men in general, or just me in particular?" At her glare, he threw up his hands in mock surrender. "Okay. But you sure do expect me to take a lot on faith." He frowned as he studied her, as if he might be thinking about something else.

"A little faith wouldn't hurt you, I'm sure. I wouldn't hurt Bea for anything in the world. She's—"

"When is that damn train coming?" Edgar had slammed a hand on the table and was glaring at Lucas and Janet.

Janet smiled at Edgar, forgetting all about the dishes and Lucas's innuendos. "It's not running today, Edgar." He looked puzzled as she led him to a chair. "How about some warm milk or hot chocolate, and we'll talk about the train schedules and how to make them better." It helped him to reminisce. She warmed milk for the hot chocolate. Clarence bestirred himself at the smell.

The older man looked at her, then Lucas, confusion ebbing from his face. "I . . . you're Lucas, Jake's boy."

Lucas nodded. "Sure am, Edgar. Haven't seen you in a long time."

Edgar slumped into a chair. "I sure do miss Jake. He was like a brother to me. You still live around these parts?"

"I live in Little Rock. I'm just visiting Mother."

Edgar sighed. "Don't know what I'd do without Bea. Just don't know what I'd do." A tear welled in the corner of his eye.

"You fish much these days, Edgar?" Lucas spoke in a quiet, gentle voice.

The man shook his head. "Can't take a boat out anymore, boy. I have trouble sometimes rememberin' things."

Janet set a steaming cup in front of Edgar. "There you go. Drink that and you'll sleep like a baby."

"Thank you, Miz Janet." He sipped at the hot chocolate, then the confusion came back into his eyes. "Back in the old days the damn trains ran on schedule." He pounded the table with his fist.

Janet sat down beside him, then remembered she'd forgotten to offer Lucas anything. Or maybe she'd forgotten on purpose, but she couldn't be bothered with niceties at the moment. If Edgar suddenly realized he'd had a lapse in front of Lucas, he'd be terribly embarrassed. "I'll talk to the engineer, Edgar, see what's happened. I'll let you know as soon as I can find out anything."

"You do that, Missy. You do that." Edgar seemed contented, sipping his chocolate and telling them about the old Kansas City Southern New Orleans Special. After a few moments Janet knew that he was aware he was telling a story. She helped him up and walked with him toward the stairs, talking all the way. When he was settled, she went back to the kitchen, hoping Lucas would have disappeared in the meantime. No such luck. She noticed he'd put all the dishes in the dishwasher and was sitting at the table, two steaming cups of chocolate before him.

"It looked so good. I haven't had hot chocolate in I don't know how long." He flashed her a grin.

Janet looked at that boyish grin and thought she might just faint and drown in her hot chocolate. One minute Mr. Macho, the next minute endearing little boy. She didn't think she could stand it. She sat down and sipped her drink, anxious to put an end to this day by retiring to her room and quietly falling apart. "This is good."

"What's wrong with Edgar?" he asked in a quiet voice. "I asked Mother, but her explanation was less than illuminating."

Janet shrugged. "I guess he pretty much went to pieces after his wife died. A year ago he had a light stroke. When he came back from the hospital, there was no one to take care of him."

Lucas frowned. "A stroke? But he's not that old."

"He's sixty-one. And it happens sometimes." She swirled the chocolate in her cup.

"Is he . . . I mean—"

"No, he's not a threat to anyone. He didn't get enough therapy after the stroke, just went home all alone. According to Bea he was living on cornflakes." She gave him a bittersweet smile. "It may not seem like it to you, but there has been a marked improvement in him over the past several weeks. Just getting him out of total isolation helped a lot. He was living in the past when I first saw him. Now he just has lapses."

Lucas leaned back in his chair and stared into his cup. "And, of course, he couldn't get disability, and he's not old enough for Medicare and Social Security. And he lost his job because he couldn't remember things and since they had to let him go, he doesn't qualify for his pension. And no insurance for therapy. Right?"

Janet's head snapped up at the bitterness in his voice. "How did you know?"

His laugh was harsh. "It's what I do for a living. I'm an administrative law judge."

She stared at him across the table. "Bea said you were a government lawyer."

"Yeah, well that pretty well sums it up. A government lawyer who tries to salvage the Edgars of the world, only to have too many decisions overturned by bureaucrats. I know all the names of the disabilities, but I only see the people once, maybe twice. Has he applied for disability under Social Security?"

"Twice. The first time he was completely lucid during the hearing. He got turned down. The last application has been pending for months." Janet shook her head sympathetically, but her thoughts were on the new version of Lucas McNair that had just popped up. She'd just assumed he was some expensive corporate lawyer. No wonder he was adamant about getting his mother somewhere safe and sound. Lucas McNair, the sensitive champion of the downtrodden, made Janet warm all over. "He'll qualify for Social Security next year, and I really think he'll totally recover, but in the meantime he can't hold a job and he can't get any help anywhere else."

Lucas grinned. "Enter Beatrice McNair, riding a white horse, Janet Gallen riding shotgun."

Janet bristled for a moment, then laughed at the image. "I guess it does kind of look like that, doesn't it?" She drained her cup. "I think I'll call it a night. Breakfast comes early in the morning."

His hand stayed her. "What about Verla?"

"She's on Supplemental Security Income. Her kids sold her place so she could qualify. They just forgot to give her the money. Stuck her in a nursing home instead, because of her arthritis. On $336 a month, she just couldn't make it out there in the workaday world alone. Anyway, they overmedicated her like crazy in the nursing home and by the time Bea rescued her, arthritis was the least of Verla's problems. She's got a long road ahead, but I'm seeing improvement, so I'm hopeful.''

Lucas shuddered. "I thought I was coming up here to get away from the grim realities of old age."

She smiled warmly and reached over and touched his arm, glad for some reason that he'd turned out to be one of the good guys instead of a tax man. "Hey, we have a lot of fun around here." Then she hurried out of the room, anxious to be alone and digest this latest information about Lucas McNair. She headed up the stairs, intent on a hot shower. Surely not even *this* man would follow her into the shower.

Thirty minutes later Janet emerged from the tiny bathroom in her robe, her hair bundled in a towel. And ran smack into Lucas, clad in Levi's and a towel around his neck. She'd thought he looked some kind of beautiful in a polo shirt, but with no shirt...well.... Janet leaned against the wall, her eyes riveted to his chest. She didn't dare look into his eyes.

"Excuse me," he murmured. "I thought you were through."

Janet had never realized just how small the attic hallway was. And it seemed to shrink by the moment. His muscular chest was covered with a dark soft mat of hair. She jammed her hands into her robe pockets to keep from touching it. "I...well, it's all yours." She wanted to rush past him, but she couldn't seem to move.

His mouth twitched into a smile. "As long as we're going to be sharing such close quarters, maybe we should declare a truce."

"Truce?" How about if she just moved to the barn for the duration.

"Truce. I don't have anything against you personally, you know, and I appreciate your being so nice to Mother. It's just that she has no business running a bed and breakfast." He moved a little closer.

Janet thought he might have quite a lot against her if she didn't move quickly. She flushed at the thought. "Oh." With that brilliant declaration, she rushed past him, trying to ignore the fact that her arm had brushed against that wonderful chest. She flung herself into her room, slamming the door behind her.

She sat for a long time in the dark, gazing out the dormer at the moonlit lake, listening to the shower start then stop. She tried her best not to think about Lucas in the shower, but it was difficult. When she heard his footsteps pause outside her door, her heart almost stopped.

Janet could practically hear him breathing on the other side of the thin wall, and she knew she had to get control of herself. She had always been a loving, gregarious woman, but what she felt around Lucas McNair was ridiculous. It was a physical response unlike any she had ever felt, and she wasn't about to let it get out of hand. Her relationship with Jack had started as a physical attraction, but she'd fallen in love. She'd been badly used, mistaking his kisses for love. That was the worst of it, she hadn't been able to see it, and she'd just tumbled deeper and deeper in love with him. And what she'd felt for Jack didn't hold a candle to what she knew she could feel for Lucas McNair.

Slipping into her bed, Janet stretched her body between the cool refreshing sheets and touched her chin where Lucas's fingers had rested. Then her lips. Then she pounded her pillow and lectured herself severely. She would *not* succumb to a physical attraction. It led to love and to hurt. And she had a feeling that Lucas was headstrong enough to use whatever means he could to get his mother into what he considered a safe situation. She would not be a part of that means, nor would she end up as part of the fallout from it.

CHAPTER FOUR

"THAT OLD CAT'S after the muffins!" Inez screamed.

Janet, who was clearing the breakfast dishes from the dining table, uttered a series of muffled oaths aimed at Clarence and Inez and hurried into the kitchen. Clarence sat in a chair at the kitchen table, his glassy eyes fixed on what was left of the blueberry muffins. Bea was upstairs showing the new guest, a Mrs. Heunfield, the finer points of crocheted snowflakes.

Janet snatched Clarence off his chair and put him behind the stove with a muffin. "Why can't you eat tuna or Little Friskies or whatever other cats eat?" Clarence grunted and fell on his muffin. She wrapped the remaining muffins and stuck them in the bread box, then turned to Inez. "There. Inez, did your mother really tell you your baby would look like a cat if you touched one?"

The girl's lower lip quivered and she nodded.

"I find that absolutely remarkable," Janet said, shaking her head. "Listen, do you want to keep an eye on Verla while I do the beds? Make sure she doesn't get trapped under her afghan?" Janet watched Inez struggle to her feet, then went off to make beds. They had been open four days now, had two guests, and

Janet was exhausted. The only bright spot in her life was the fact that Lucas had only been around at mealtime, and she'd been too tired to pay any attention to him. Well, maybe she noticed him—just a little—and maybe she did think about him occasionally at night, in the quiet, with only a thin wall between them. He had made several trips to Rogers, and he spent hours fiddling around with the boats, particularly with one she thought was a sailboat. From her one trip to the boat dock, she thought they all looked flimsy and unreliable.

The rest of the time he wandered around looking smug. But Janet was sure that his very presence was the major cause of her exhaustion. Pounding hearts and stomachs in constant revolt did tend to wear one out. She kept thinking things would settle down to a routine, but with Inez, Verla and Edgar, they never did. The bed and breakfast alone would be no problem, the old folks by themselves would be no problem, but the combination was a real killer. She worried constantly. For the first time, she began to have twinges of doubt about the whole operation, which of course were overwhelmed by twinges of guilt over the twinges of doubt. "Rats," she muttered, snapping a sheet onto the bed, "you're just having a bad day. If number one son wasn't prowling around, there wouldn't be a problem. It's all his fault." She decided a walk in the woods might help *her* outlook. She looked up from the bed as Bea bustled in.

"Oh, let me help you with that, dear."

"I can handle it, Bea."

"I know you can, but you must be worn out. You've been doing entirely too much."

Janet smiled and declined to point out that they couldn't just ignore the work if they were going to make a success of the business. "It will all settle down soon."

"Oh, dear, you're not having a good day. I can tell."

"Well, I have had better ones. I'm just antsy about everything."

"I know just the thing, my dear. You need a good workout. We all do. We haven't had one in days." The older woman beamed with excitement.

"I don't know, Bea." If there was anything Janet wasn't too excited about right now, it was a good workout. She was too darned tired. She had started Bea and Edgar and Verla on a low impact aerobics program when she first arrived, thinking it would help detoxify Verla and speed up Edgar's recovery. She felt a twinge of guilt that she had been remiss the past few days. "Maybe you're right."

"Of course I'm right, dear. I'll get Verla and Edgar."

Janet hurried to her attic room and threw on a bodysuit and running shorts. When she came downstairs, Bea had Bob Wills and the Texas Playboys blaring throughout the house. Janet preferred the Pointer Sisters, but Bea said she remembered dancing to Bob Wills and crew all those years ago. She led her class through a series of gentle stretching exercises, then began marching them around the living room. Verla's cotton housedress flapped around her thin legs.

"Deep breaths," she shouted over the strains of "San Antonio Rose." "Deep, deep, deep. Let's get some blood to our brain. March, march, march. Stop. Arm circles, round and round. Step right, step left, right, left. Good. March." Janet thought it must be quite a sight, with Edgar in his overalls and the women in their housedresses, but they seemed to enjoy it, and she did too, once she got started. And she did think it helped them. Bea sang along to the record and Verla hummed out the tune, although Janet didn't think her tune had anything to do with the record. "Down on the floor. Easy, Verla, don't hurry. Lift one leg at a time. Right, left, right, left." While she kept them doing slow leg lifts, she pushed herself up on her shoulders and did bicycles. It felt good to stretch her tensed muscles. "Right, left, right, left," she chanted, bicycling away.

"Very pretty," a soft voice behind her said.

She jerked around too fast to see who it was and fell over sideways. Not that she needed to look. From her ungainly sprawl, she saw Lucas leaning against the door, grinning—and staring. "Everybody up. March." When she got her little class up and moving, she marched past him. "Go away. You're disrupting my class. Let's move those arms."

"Oh, Lucas, dear, you must try this," Bea cried. "It's so invigorating. It makes one feel ethereal."

Lucas fell into line behind Janet. "Good idea. Helps the old blood supply to the brain, right?"

"Right. I mean left, right. Arm circles." She turned to him as she marched. "Go away," she whispered.

"But Mother insisted."

"She's not running the class. March. High steps, Edgar."

Bea stopped dead in her tracks. "Oh, Lucas, dear, I meant to tell you—"

Before Janet could catch herself, she crashed into Bea, grabbing to steady the older woman, managing to fall backward in the process. She felt strong arms circle her waist and burn through the thin bodysuit. "Oh. Oh!"

"Nice."

She struggled to extract herself from his clutches. "March or get out," she commanded with all the authority her squeaky voice could manage.

He threw up his hands in mock surrender. "I'm going, I'm going." He gave her a parting wink. "Very nice."

Janet flipped off the record player. "That's good for today. Let's walk and cool off." She led them in a few stretches and turned them loose. She wanted to get away from everybody and everything—and concentrate on the band of heat still burning around her middle.

Bea smiled and stretched. "I feel quite rejuvenated. I must see about lunch."

"Bea, we just had breakfast."

"I know, but dear Lucas does like a nice hot lunch."

Janet thought about suggesting that if dear Lucas liked a nice hot lunch, he could darn well fix it. "Right. I think I'll go outside and cool off." The beds were made, her charges were exercised, why not? Neither of the guests seemed to be about. She poured a cup of coffee and wondered where they were off to.

Pete Bradley spent most of his time either in his room or wandering around with an enormous sketch pad, all of which Janet was grateful for. His few demands were simple. Janet had more reservations about the new guest, Mrs. Heunfield. She seemed a nice enough matronly type, but Janet got the distinct impression that the woman was not above getting nasty if she thought she wasn't getting her money's worth, which was probably never. She had that look about her.

She fled to the backyard with her cup of strong coffee and collapsed in the chaise longue to regroup and cool off—more from Lucas than the exercise, she was afraid. It was a beautiful spring day, mild and bright. The first honeybees buzzed about, searching for early blooms. Robins strutted around the yard, cocking their heads to listen, then frantically pecking at the earth for food. Janet leaned back and relaxed with the gentle sounds of spring.

"If you don't mind my saying so, you look a little on the frazzled side again."

She jerked up straight, almost dumping her coffee down her front. She'd assumed he'd gone off somewhere. Like to town. Evidently he'd been lurking, waiting to pounce on her. She nonchalantly tried to cover her front by crossing her arms. "I'm fine."

Lucas lounged against the oak tree, all cool and comfortable in his starched Levi's and polo shirt. Of course, he hadn't been doing aerobics and chasing Clarence and making beds and looking for Verla's afghan, which she had stuffed behind the wardrobe for fear some of these new, strange people might steal it.

Janet made a mental note to talk to the doctor and see if they could hurry Verla's recovery in some way.

He sat down in the lawn chair beside her. "Is it occurring to you that this whole thing just might not be working?"

She flushed and concentrated on a bee busily working a bright yellow dandelion flower. "No, it is not. Things are going just fine. I'd better go help Bea with lunch."

He stayed her with a hand on her arm. "Finish your coffee." He leaned back in his chair. "You need more help for one thing. At least until your maid gets back on her feet." He waited for a response, but none came. "I've been doing a few calculations. I don't see any way this place can hope to turn a profit in the foreseeable future."

Janet bridled. Every time he came around, she either got mad or tingly. It was wearing. "Well, we did a few calculations before we started it, and we can make it. Not much profit, admittedly, but the operation will pay its way." Assuming Bea didn't visit any more of her friends in the nursing home and whisk them back to Crow's Rest.

He laughed and propped his feet on the foot of her lounge. "That's because you haven't had sufficient exposure to Mother's particular brand of financial management."

She awkwardly tucked her feet and legs underneath her to avoid touching him and wished she'd stopped to put on more clothes. "Which is?"

"I'm sure, even as we speak, that Mom is figuring out reasons why none of the guests should be expected to pay. She is saying to herself how tacky it is to take money for something she enjoys doing so much. At the very least, she's apologizing for taking their money." He stared toward the woods, a peculiar expression on his face.

Janet winced. She had seen signs of that sort of thing in Bea, and there had been some spirited discussions about room rates, but she had been firm. "Well, that really isn't a problem. I take care of guest registration and checkout. I was very firm with Bea on that issue, and she turned the money taking over to me entirely. Believe me, anyone who stays at Crow's Rest pays. Now, I really must go." She struggled to get out of the lounge. His long legs trapped her very neatly unless she wanted to vault over the back. In which case she would undoubtedly crash and burn.

"I also had a long talk with Mom's doctor yesterday."

"Oh? You have been busy." She sipped cold coffee and considered a leap over his legs—except her feet had gone to sleep or something. His seeing Bea's doctor explained at least some of his trips to town. She wondered what other little surprises he had in mind. He'd probably turned Clarence in to the Health Department, too. She wiggled her toes until her feet began to tingle.

"Yes. She's still a potential heart attack candidate, as I'm sure you know. The medication has not been totally successful in controlling her blood pressure or the angina."

"I know all that, but I repeat. She's had fewer angina attacks in the past month than in the past year. I keep very close tabs on her blood pressure and make sure she takes her medicine." She knew where this was all leading. Whisk City. "And I'm careful she doesn't overexert herself."

"Yes, I know. But the fact remains, it could happen anytime."

Janet sat up straight and tried to untangle her tingly feet, anger beginning to replace her tiredness. "It could happen to any of us at any time. I happen to think it will happen much later to Bea if she's doing what she loves."

"And in the meantime you're going to kill yourself just to prove the point?"

"I'm fine. I thrive on hard work. In fact—" she waved a hand at the side yard, searching for some project to demonstrate her love of hard work, knowing full well she was getting ready to fall in a trap—or through the looking glass again. She pointed to the general vicinity of a long-forgotten garden. "I'm thinking about putting in a garden, I have so much spare time." Janet heard the words, but didn't believe she'd said them. She couldn't even keep a philodendron alive.

"Really?" He grinned and his eyes twinkled. "I think you might find it difficult to hoe your radishes by moonlight."

She jumped up and almost fell over him. "I like fresh vegetables."

He reached up to steady her, a mischievous grin spreading over his face. "Well, maybe I could help you with a garden."

Visions of him tending the garden in cutoffs and no shirt wafted through her senses. "Oh, I doubt it. You don't seem like the gardening type."

He stood and laid his arm on her shoulder, his hand resting on the back of her neck. "Just what type do I seem, Janet?"

His eyes held hers. Something flickered deep in those dark, shadowy eyes. "Oh, I don't know. Racquetball or something. Why don't you go sail your boat? You just have time before lunch."

He drew her closer. "Are you trying to get rid of me? I'll have you know Dad and I had the best garden in this part of the world. We took blue ribbons every year at the county fair for our squash," he said confidentially.

"Squash?" Her heart pounded wildly as his hand rubbed her neck. It felt wonderful—and she wished he would stop. He was much nicer when he was mad than when he was nice, she thought, or something like that. He was nothing but trouble, yet she gave herself to the magical fingers massaging her neck.

"We were known as the squash kings of Benton county," he whispered, his voice soft and silky as a new kitten. His lips were inches from her ear. "One year we had a forty-pound butternut."

His hand caressed her neck, and visions of the giant squash and the proud boy waltzed through her head. "Forty pounds," she whispered helplessly, leaning into the gentle hand on her neck.

"It was a beautiful squash. Almost as beautiful as you are." He pulled her against him.

A gentle finger trailed down her cheek as he held her against his hard body. "Beautiful squash," she said dreamily.

"Beautiful Janet." His lips brushed her cheek.

"Beautiful Janet." His lips brushed hers before she realized what he'd said, what she'd said; what he'd done, what she'd done. "What?" She pushed away from him, her cheeks flushed, her body warm. "What do you think you're doing?"

His eyes held hers, swirling with dark desire. He grinned and reached up to push a wisp of hair away from her face. "I thought we were discussing squash."

"Ohhhh, pooh on your squash. I have to go help Bea with your *nice hot lunch*." She stalked to the house, ignoring his laughter, stumbling twice on her tingly feet.

"Janet dear," Bea said, looking up when Janet opened the door. "I was digging in the freezer and guess what I found?" Bea held out a package of something.

"What?" She was in no mood for guessing games. She was hot and bothered and her feet felt as though they were falling off.

"Some nice butternut squash. I'm fixing squash pie for supper."

"Oh, how could you, Bea?" Janet wailed.

"Don't you like squash pie, dear? Oh, you should have seen the lovely squash Lucas and his father used to grow. One can hardly tell squash pie from pumpkin pie, and everyone likes pumpkin pie. It's so...American."

Janet slammed pots and pans, glared at Inez and wondered briefly if the girl was sleeping in the kitchen. She seemed to be there all the time. Scooter hid under his chair. "Pumpkins and squash are not the same thing. And I've heard all about the forty-pound squash."

"Oh, but they are related. I'm sure you'll love it." She stood still, a finger on her cheek. "You know, I think the purple ribbon for that squash is somewhere in the attic. I must look for it."

"I don't think she cares much for squash, Mother." Lucas stood in the door, his jaw muscles twitching.

"How extraordinary," Bea exclaimed.

"I love squash," Janet said through clenched teeth. "Now I really must go change."

"Too bad. I like your exercise attire." Lucas grinned as his eyes trailed over her scantily clad body.

"Oh, not just yet, dear." Bea sat down at the table with a cup of tea and a sigh. "Sit down, you two. I must tell you about the most marvelous thing."

Lucas poured coffee, rummaged in the refrigerator for cream and sat down. Janet poured coffee and leaned against the wood stove, as far away from Lucas as she could get and still stay in the kitchen, arms hugged tightly across her bodysuit. Her face felt as hot as if the old stove were going full steam.

"After I got Mrs. Heunfield straight on her snowflakes—my dears, you simply wouldn't believe the mess she'd made of them. She was using a triple crochet instead of a double, and a G hook, and of course the snowflakes were big enough for tablecloths. She and Verla must have gone to the same school. Well, I hope I've got her straightened out now, but I do have serious doubts about her efforts. She just doesn't seem to have the knack. It's all in the fingers, you know. I really think she's more the cross-stitch type." Bea sipped her tea breathlessly.

"About the marvelous thing, Bea," Janet gently reminded her, having visions of the story lasting well through lunch and into the afternoon. She was feeling more naked by the minute.

"Oh. Yes. Well, I stopped in to see if Mr. Bradley needed anything. Such a nice young man. Well, he's so taken with the place, he's going to paint it. I mean a picture of it."

Lucas turned in his chair to stare at Janet. She slid down the stove a little. "That's nice," he said, staring at Janet's legs. "But don't get your hopes up. He's probably just a weekend artist."

Bea laughed. "Oh, Lucas, you are such a pessimist at times. He's *very* well known. He's had shows in Tulsa and Kansas City. He gets quite a lot of money for his paintings."

"Really?" Lucas sipped coffee and studied Janet's feet.

"That's why it's so marvelous. He's agreed to trade a month's lodging for the painting."

Janet choked on her coffee and made the mistake of looking at Lucas. He covered what she knew was a broad grin with a hand and his coffee cup and seemed to be twitching all over. "How clever of you, Mother. Don't you think so, Janet?"

"I shall hang it over the fireplace," Bea said proudly.

Janet shot a withering look at Lucas, whose twitching got worse. His eyes were sending messages of "I told you so." "Bea, I thought we agreed that all the guests would pay."

"Well, it's all the same, my dear. The painting is just like money."

"See? I told you Mother was a financial wizard," Lucas said, unable to restrain his laughter another minute. He leaned over and bussed Bea on the cheek.

At that moment Edgar arrived and announced that if they planned to ride on his New Orleans Special, they'd better get their behinds on the train. He didn't hold his trains for anyone.

Janet could have kissed Edgar for the distraction. She hurried to his side. "We can't possibly get away today, Edgar. Let's take a little walk." She took his arm and led him toward the front door.

"Miz Janet?" he said, confusion written all over his face.

"Yes. Did you know the dogwood in the front yard is in full bloom?"

"It is, isn't it."

"Let's pick a few blooms for the table, shall we?"

"I'd like that."

As they picked the lovely ivory blooms, Janet talked calmly and by the time they had arranged the blossoms in a bowl on the table, he was back in the present and asking about the young man sitting in the yard drawing. She fixed Edgar some hot tea and settled him in the porch swing to watch Pete Bradley sketch. She wanted very much to rant and rave at the artist and accuse him of trying to bilk an old lady out of room and board, but she knew deep down that it was Bea who had talked *him* into the deal. She would have to pore over the budget tonight and make adjustments.

When she finally returned to the kitchen, Lucas and Bea were deep in conversation, all smiles. Janet's suspicion leaped to the fore. She could tell by Bea's sudden flush that they were planning something that involved her—something she wasn't going to like. "Well, Edgar is all settled on the porch," she reported, mostly to have something to say.

"That's nice," Bea said. "Lucas and I have just been talking about how hard you work, dear. We—"

"Mother and I have decided you need a little break from things."

"I'm fine. I don't need a break." She glared at him.

"Of course you do, my dear. Lucas is going to take you out for a nice sail this afternoon."

Janet's eyes widened. "In a boat?"

Lucas sprawled smugly in his chair. "Sailing *is* generally done in a boat. Or do you sail some other way?"

"I don't sail. I mean, I don't do boats." She felt the familiar tension rise at the mention of boats.

Lucas sat up straight, sudden interest in his face. "You don't *do* boats? What on earth does that mean?"

She busied herself with moving plates from the cabinet to the table and back again. "It means just what it sounds like."

"Mother, I do believe we have found something our invincible Janet is afraid of."

Bea looked perplexed. "What a strange thing. Did a boat scare you as a child, dear?"

Janet flushed. "It's a long story."

Lucas stood up. "You're afraid of the water aren't you?" He sounded incredulous.

"Not exactly. It's just that there's such a lot of it in a lake." She began rearranging the silverware.

Bea worried at the tablecloth. "This is most distressing. One can't possibly enjoy living on a lake if one is afraid of water."

"Certainly not," Lucas chimed in. "I think it's our duty to help her conquer this fear."

"I don't have to get in the water to enjoy it," Janet wailed, but she knew they would never let it rest. "And I'm not getting in any sailboat. They lean too much—generally right before they fall over."

Lucas took her arm. "How about flat bottom boats? They're safe, and we'll go slow."

"Well . . ." She didn't want to get in any boat, particularly not with him.

"There are some really beautiful places out there," he murmured in her ear.

"And Lucas is ever so careful with boats, Janet. It will do you all the good in the world. Water is so calming."

Janet saw nothing at all calming about water unless it was in a bathtub or an aquarium, but she knew there was no graceful way to get out of it. And she wasn't about to be humiliated by Lucas carrying her kicking and screaming out to a boat, which she had no doubt he would do. "Oh, all right. Just for an hour. I have work to do."

"Great. Go change into something . . . a little more boaty." His voice and eyes teased.

Janet went to her room, dragging her feet every step of the way, wondering if they would find it strange if she were to just disappear out the window. Of course, Mr. Macho would track her down and drag her to his boat. It had been so easy to ignore her fear of water while she stayed in Little Rock. There were few occasions when she was even around water. Lucas was right. Water was about the only thing she was afraid of. She'd looked at the lake many times in the past few weeks and wished she could enjoy it—really enjoy it.

She dressed in old jeans and the sloppiest sweatshirt she could find and wished she had some Valium. Lucas would no doubt take great delight in careening the boat and scaring her silly. She would no doubt see the *real* Lucas McNair today. Well, it was time to face up to it. As she walked back down the stairs, she had a feeling this was going to be the longest hour of her life.

CHAPTER FIVE

"YOU MUST HAVE forty pounds of clothes on," Lucas said, trying to hide a grin. "You'd sink like a rock."

Janet ignored the grin—and the ragged cutoffs and sleeveless T-shirt. "I thought you said the boat was safe."

"It is."

"Then why are you talking about sinking?" She walked onto the boat dock and looked at the boat. It was a little wooden thing, pointed at the front, but fairly wide at the middle. It did look safer than a sailboat, still...

"Joke. It was a joke." He handed her a life jacket.

She peeked into the boat house to see if any of the other boats looked safer. They didn't. "Why do you have so many boats?"

"When you live on water, you collect boats. The aluminum flat bottom was for the river. Dad and I made this little jewel." He pointed to the wooden boat.

"You made it?" She was going out in all that water in a homemade boat?

"Well, all boats are made by someone. This is a very well-designed, well-built boat. It took us one whole winter to build it."

"How old is it?" she asked suspiciously. Nothing like a first ride in an *old*, homemade boat.

"It's been well cared for, don't worry." He helped her into the life jacket and tied it securely around her. "You really are afraid, aren't you?"

"No. I always shake like this." She looked up and saw something like real concern in his eyes—which made her feel all the worse. She was fully prepared for him to tease her unmercifully and scare the stuffing out of her. She was not prepared for any real concern about her phobia. She didn't want sympathy and concern, she wanted . . . oh, she didn't know what she wanted, except for it to be over with.

"Look, we don't really have to do this." He held her upper arms and scanned her face.

She refused to look at him. She also refused to be the object of his sympathy. "Yes we do. I've put it off for a lot of years." He handed her down into the boat, which rocked. Her stomach rocked right along with it.

"Okay. I hope you learn to like it. There are some beautiful places on this lake. Places you can't see except from the water." He stepped into the boat. "You want to face front or back?"

"Front." She couldn't very well sit facing him with her eyes closed. "I like to see disaster before it strikes."

He placed a hand on her shoulder. "Nothing's going to happen." He started the electric trolling motor, and the boat quietly slipped away from the dock. "How did you get so scared of water?"

Janet clutched the sides of the boat, white-knuckled, peeked out at the lake, then closed her eyes again, trying to ignore the rocking motion. "When I was a kid—maybe ten—we were doing belly flops and just as I jumped, my brother grabbed my ankles. It scared me and when I hit the water, I gulped in several gallons."

"That's a heck of a thing to happen to a kid," he said quietly.

"I came to, draped over a dog house, spitting and doing all those other nice things people do when their lungs are full of water."

"You could have drowned. Was it on a lake? Is that why you're so afraid of this one?"

She was silent for a while, then let out a long, quivering sigh. "No, it was a backyard pool with about three feet of water in it." She imagined she heard a stifled laugh. "Well, if I can almost drown in three feet of water, do you think I'm safe in hundreds of feet of it? I mean, that's the humiliating part."

"And you haven't been in water since?"

"No."

"Well, I think we can take care of your little phobia. Did you like the water before it happened?"

"Loved it."

"Good. We'll go out for a small run every day, and I predict that within two weeks, you'll wonder why you were ever afraid." She shrugged her shoulders under the sloppy sweatshirt. "By the way, you won't be as queasy if you open your eyes."

Her eyes popped open. "How did you know my eyes were closed?" She turned to look at him but didn't let go her iron grip.

"It's what people do when they're scared."

"Oh." Why did he have to be so perceptive? Why couldn't he be a jerk and laugh at her fears instead of trying to treat them? But she did look around long enough to see that they were very close to the shore. It made her feel better. The way her adrenaline was pumping, she could probably run to shore from here—right on top of the water.

"I'm going to take you to a place that will make you know the trip was worth it."

"Where?" She doubted that the Eiffel Tower would be worth the trip if she had to go by boat.

"You'll see."

Within minutes he turned the boat into a sheltered cove. On the right, a limestone bluff rose a hundred feet. On the left, a sea of dogwood, interspersed with enormous white oak trees gently edged the lake. She was glad her eyes were open. She couldn't remember when she had seen anything so beautiful. The beauty of the hillside took her mind off the boat and she forgot to hold on. "It's lovely."

"I thought you might like it." He nudged the boat in to shore and jumped out to secure it. "We'll stay here long enough for you to start breathing again."

She climbed out of the boat and sighed as her feet hit solid ground. "I've never seen so many dogwoods in one place." She rushed to a gnarled tree and kissed the rough bark.

"If that's gratitude for arriving safely, you might lavish it on the one who got you here."

She looked up. He was leaning against another tree, arms crossed, a gentle smile on his face. Her heart, which had just begun to settle down from the boat ride, started pounding again. What was she doing, alone in the middle of the woods with him? In the middle of these lovely, spring-blossoming woods, which conjured up all sorts of...thoughts. She decided to keep the conversation to trees and water and all those other neutral things. She slid to the ground, her back to the tree, and looked out over the lake. She had to admit, it was beautiful. "Have the dogwoods always been here?"

He came and sat beside her. "Uh-huh. If you walked right out into the lake, oh, about a hundred yards, you'd be standing in what used to be the apple orchard. We cut firewood on this hillside, but Dad would never cut a dogwood. He considered it a crime against nature to cut a dogwood, because of the legend."

She vaguely remembered something about a dogwood legend, but couldn't remember the details. Actually she could hardly remember her name at the moment, surrounded by the beauty of the place and the closeness of the man. "I guess I knew it at one time, but—"

"Supposedly the dogwood was used to make the cross for Christ's crucifixion. That's why it's gnarled now, so it can't ever be used for that purpose again. Dad loved that legend. He used to point out the oldest dogwoods, show me how twisted they were."

"That's really nice." She watched him reach up and gently trace the twisted pattern of bark.

"Yeah. He was a nice man. Anyway, by getting rid of most of the oak on this hillside, the dogwoods took it for their own. He left enough white oak to shelter them from the wind and summer heat. Dogwoods like a little shade in the summer, you know." His voice was soft as he talked about another time.

"It must have been a lovely farm." She picked up a twig and began to break it into tiny pieces and felt a strange peacefulness settle over her.

"It was. I love the lake, but it was hard to see water gradually creep up and take the orchard and the hay meadows. Dad put a lot of work into this place. I don't think he ever really got over the presence of the lake. It was like he didn't have anything to do after the lake filled."

"I wish I could have known him. Bea talks about him a lot."

Lucas laughed softly, his long, tanned legs resting beside hers. "I wish Dad could have lived to see Mom and her new enterprise. He would have sucked on his pipe a few times real hard, rumbled in his throat and said, 'The old girl's kicked over the traces, by God.'"

Janet laughed and tossed her broken twigs down, then picked up another one. "It's too bad he didn't have a hobby or something to take his mind off the lake and his lost farm."

"Oh, he tried a dozen things over the years, finally went to work in town for a while. That's the problem with devoting your life to work. You don't know what to do when it's over."

Janet heard a tinge of bitterness to the words and wondered if Lucas had hobbies that would sustain him when his work was over. She somehow suspected he didn't, any more than she did.

"How could you ever stand to leave it?" She could easily sit in the midst of these trees for the rest of her life—particularly with Lucas. She squirmed nervously at that thought.

He shrugged. "You know how it is with kids. Wherever they are, they can't wait till they can be somewhere else. I guess you think this is heaven after growing up in the city, right?"

"Right." The smell of the humus beneath the trees wafted up to her nostrils and mixed with the scent of his after-shave. Janet thought she'd never smelled anything so lovely.

"That's because you don't know how tough it can be trying to live off the land. Late frosts, insects, all the things just waiting to take your crop. I didn't have what it takes. And Rogers wasn't exactly filled with bright lights and career opportunities when I got my law degree."

Janet plucked a dogwood blossom from a branch above her and touched it to her cheek, fascinated with its leathery, yet velvety texture. "Didn't you ever want to come back?"

Lucas laughed. "Every time I came to visit. But I guess I'm a city boy now. I don't think you can ever go back. Somebody famous said that, didn't they? You can't ever go home? I guess they were right."

Janet felt a stab of disappointment. He looked so right with the woods and the lake. And she felt so right with him. She shook herself, determined to get on some other subject—some subject that would bring out the jerk in him, not the nostalgia. "Have you figured out a way to close us down yet?" The laughter she expected didn't come.

"Nope. I'm not even sure I'm looking right now."

She sat up straight and turned to stare at him. "You're not?"

"These things have a way of taking care of themselves." He leaned over and stuck a blossom in her hair.

"What does that mean?" She pulled away from the hand that lingered in her hair, more suspicious now than she'd been when he was determined to close them. But at least it took her mind off...other things.

"Just what it says. How come you never married?" He was lying down, propped on one elbow, drawing circles on her jeaned leg with a twig.

She wanted to move away but didn't. "No one's ever asked, if you have to know."

"Including the one you were running away from when you came up here?" He looked up and smiled.

"What makes you think I was running away from anything?" She struggled to keep her hand from moving up to stroke his hair.

"It's pretty obvious. A doctor? Intern?"

"Resident, and I don't want to talk about it."

"Fine." He was now tracing lines up her arm with his twig. "But I can't see you burying yourself forever in a do-it-yourself old folks' home."

"Nothing is forever," she said, concentrating on the intricate twig drawings on her arm, wishing she hadn't worn the heavy sweatshirt.

"Some things are."

His finger had replaced the twig and was now tracing delicate patterns on her cheek. When he touched her ear, she jumped and realized what he was doing. She scooted around the tree. "Well. And why aren't you married?"

He laughed and flopped down on his back. "I thought we were talking about you."

"*You* were talking about me." She peeked around the tree, knowing she had to get away from him before something happened that she would regret.

"I was married."

"Oh." She got up and walked farther into the woods. He followed.

"Don't you want to know what happened?"

"No."

"Okay." He stopped and studied a tender fern which the warm spring weather had coaxed out of its winter sleep.

"What."

"I thought you didn't want to know."

"I don't." She stopped to touch the trunk of a dogwood tree, rubbing her fingers against the rough surface. She inhaled deeply of the warm, earthy woods smell.

"I was supposed to become a wealthy tax attorney. I found out I hated tax law. I never saw anyone but IRS auditors. Anyway, I decided to try for an administrative law judge position. She discovered she liked wealthy tax attorneys better than poor law judges."

"Oh." Janet rubbed the rough bark until her fingers felt tingly, trying to take her mind off Lucas and the woods and the quiet and the strange feelings about to overwhelm her.

"Did anyone ever tell you that you're a really scintillating conversationalist?"

"Jack discovered dermatologists don't marry nurses if they want wealthy practices in Houston." There, she'd said it. He lifted her hand from the bark and touched each finger with a feather-light kiss.

"I'm sorry."

"Yeah, so was I." She turned and his lips touched hers. A fire caught deep inside her and began to spread. She felt his lean body press against her, felt the heat through her heavy shirt. His lips teased and questioned. She felt herself respond and tried to pull back. "We shouldn't...."

He trailed kisses down her throat. "Why not, Janet? You feel the same thing I do."

"No, I—" This time his kiss demanded, leaving her breathless when he stopped.

"Are you telling me you don't feel anything?"

He tilted her face up, and she saw the desire flickering in his dark eyes. It would be so easy, so nice...

"I think we'd better get back."

He stroked her cheek with a finger. "He must have really hurt you."

"I...he did." *And I don't intend to let it happen again,* she thought as the old hurt welled up. It would be so easy to love this man, and so hard to live with the hurt when he left.

"I wouldn't ever hurt you," he murmured against her ear.

How many times had Jack told her that? She pushed him away and clung to the dogwood tree. "Well, it certainly is lovely here," she said with a brightness she didn't feel. "But we'd better go. It's almost teatime."

He looked at her for a long moment, then slapped the tree with his hand. "Teatime. Right." He took her hand and led her, none too gently, back to the boat.

She wondered what he was so mad about now. She took her seat and grabbed the sides of the boat as he shoved it into the water and jumped in. She hardly noticed the rocking motion. She sat rigid, facing straight ahead. "Look, I think it would be better if we...you know, didn't, umm, I mean, don't you think this might be a conflict of interest?" She didn't trust herself to be the one to say no—she had to head him off before anything started.

"That's not exactly how I would describe it." His voice sounded hard and angry. "Just forget it. It won't happen again."

Janet should have been relieved, but instead she felt a twinge of disappointment. She stared straight ahead and wondered what was going on in his head. She wanted to turn and see his face but didn't.

"What all do you want in the garden?" he asked after a long while, his voice back to its normal, teasing quality.

"The garden?"

"The garden. You know, the one you want because you have so much spare time? I'm going into town this evening to get the seed. I think I can borrow a tiller from down the road."

She didn't want to discuss gardens; she wanted to know what he was thinking. Now that she was far enough away from him to think, she could go back to some of her other thousand or so worries. "Why are you doing this? I know you haven't given up on moving Bea to Little Rock."

"Let's just say one has to make adjustments from time to time in one's plans."

"I wish you'd stop talking in riddles."

"Oh, I think it would be a real drawing card to serve fresh vegetables to the guests. You know, we could turn the old barn into a really nice facility, add eight or ten rooms."

She whirled around, totally forgetting to hang on. "Are you telling me you not only approve the operation but want to expand it?" She didn't believe that for a moment.

"Of course, it would take a considerable investment and a lot of work."

"You're planning something, I know you are. And it's not going to work. We're very happy just the way we are."

"What a suspicious mind you have, my dear." He steered the boat toward the dock and in minutes had bumped it and secured a line. "Now, that wasn't so bad, was it?"

Janet was relieved to be back on solid ground but also pleased that the return trip had not been nearly so hair-raising as the trip out. What had been hair-raising was what had happened in the woods—what she'd felt, which was the first step on the road to disaster. "I guess not." But she was hardly listening to him.

When they started for the house, Pete Bradley called from his chair in front of the house. They walked toward him. "Can I do something for you, Mr. Bradley?" Janet asked.

"Pete. Just Pete. The old fellow? One on the swing?"

"Yes?" Janet glanced toward the porch swing, where Edgar was swinging and looking very agitated.

"What's with him? Spent half the afternoon hanging over my shoulder, talking about some damn train."

Her temper flared. "Mr. Bradley, all of us become forgetful if we live long enough. It does not mean we are dangerous, which is what you're implying. Believe me, Edgar means no harm to you or anyone else." She turned to go, angry at the artist, angry at herself for going off joyriding with Lucas. It would not have happened if she'd been here.

"Well, hard to concentrate on work with him hanging around."

Janet whirled, her tenuous control gone. "Oh, why don't you—go study an English book. Learn to put subjects in your sentences." She hurried toward the house, Lucas right behind.

"What happened to your 'the customer is always right' philosophy of management?"

"Oh, shut up." It was all his fault anyway. If she hadn't been so rattled over him, she never would have lost her temper.

"We could throw the rascal out. It's not like he's paying rent or anything, thanks to Mom."

"I hope he ends up drooling down his shirt—at age thirty-five." She slammed into the house. When she got to the kitchen, Bea was nowhere to be seen, Clarence was sitting licking the icing on a corner of a cake and Inez was huddled in her chair, weeping as if the world would end before tea. Janet made choking sounds, and Lucas leaned against the door, hand over his mouth, jaw twitching.

"I couldn't help it, Janet. He wouldn't go away," Inez wailed.

"Of course he won't go away. You have to pick him up and make him go away." She snatched Clarence off the table and almost flung him in the direction of his Dutch oven. He let out a howl almost as loud as Inez. "Where's Bea?"

"I don't know. There was a ruckus upstairs."

Bea swept into the kitchen, her face flushed. She had Verla by the hand. "Inez, why don't you help Verla with her afghan or something?"

Inez dried her tears and took the old woman by the hand. "Verla, I'm having lots of trouble with my stitches. I just can't seem to—"

"Inez, honey." Verla's face lit up and her eyes cleared. "I've been looking all over for you. I've just remembered what we're doing wrong on the blanket." She turned and looked at Bea. "Oh, Bea, did I have another spell?'' Her face crinkled as if she might cry.

"Just a tiny one. It's all right, dear,'' Bea assured her and shooed them out of the kitchen.

Janet sighed. "I don't understand why Inez is so calm and cool and wonderful with Verla and so darned hysterical about everything else. Now. What happened, Bea?''

The older woman smoothed her hair and put water on to boil. "Nothing. Nothing at all.''

Janet looked at Lucas and saw the concern in his eyes. "Sit down, Bea. Let's check your blood pressure.''

"Nonsense, dear. There's nothing wrong with my blood pressure. It's just that Verla is a bit tiring at times.''

Janet thought that might be the understatement of the century. She led Bea to a chair and took the blood pressure equipment out of a cupboard. She quickly checked the pressure and found it slightly elevated. Something had happened to upset Bea. "What upset you, Bea?''

"Nothing, my dear. I'm quite all right now. Did you and Lucas have a nice outing?''

Lucas grinned. "Charming. I took her to the dogwood hill.''

"Oh, I haven't been there for years. Isn't it lovely?''

Janet wrapped her stethoscope around the cuff and put them away. "It's very nice.''

"How did you do with the boat? And the water?'' Bea's concern was real.

"Just fine.'' Janet busied herself with the tea things.

"Isn't Lucas wonderful with boats?"

"Wonderful," she said wearily, thinking he was better with seduction than with boats.

Bea jumped up. "Well, I must get tea together."

Janet gently pushed her back into her chair. "Sit. I'll take care of tea."

"Oh I can't let you do that, dear."

"Lucas, take Bea into the sitting room and entertain her. Sit on her if you have to. I'll have things ready in a minute."

"Will do. Come on, Mother."

"Isn't she just wonderful, Lucas?" Bea asked as she left the room.

"She certainly is, Mother, but she seems a little bit upset. I guess it's the excitement of the boat." He laughed.

Janet boiled water and surgically removed Clarence's part of the cake. She threw together some little sandwiches and fumed. Fumed about whatever had upset Bea, fumed about that awful artist, fumed about what had happened in the woods. She wanted to know why Lucas had suddenly changed his mind about things, and what all his cryptic little bits of wisdom meant. She had no doubt they meant something, just as she had no doubt he still planned to get rid of her and whisk Bea off. He'd just come up with some sneaky way to do it—maybe making her fall in love with him so she'd agree to anything he wanted. She winced at the thought, knowing that a few more episodes of concern, sympathy and hot kisses from him would certainly do the trick.

In the meantime, there was Edgar. It had simply not occurred to her that he would present problems with the guests. Well, surprise. The burning question was, what was she going to do about it? His progress could only continue if he were in normal surroundings, around people. And she strongly suspected that whatever had upset Bea had to do with Verla and Mrs. Heunfield. She would have to come up with some way to deal with the problem before it got out of hand—like her problem with Lucas was getting out of hand.

She poured boiling water over the tea and snatched up the tray. She would worry about all that tomorrow.

CHAPTER SIX

JANET AWOKE to the sound of an awful clattering engine. She peeked out from under the covers just long enough to determine that it was barely daylight, then pulled them back over her head, cursing whoever was making all the racket, knowing full well it could only be Lucas.

She'd spent a miserable night, tossing and turning and worrying about what to do about virtually everything in the world. And had come to the conclusion that there were no solutions. She finally threw the covers off and went down to the second floor where she could see the side yard from the empty guest room.

She sat down on the edge of the bed and leaned over to look out. The sun had just popped over the hills to the east of the lake. It cast a rosy pink glow on the scene below her. Lucas was following a bucking Rototiller. He wore a pair of flimsy running shorts, a snug white T-shirt and shoes with no socks. His arm and shoulder muscles were knotted with tension as the tiller jerked and bounced over the sod. His legs seemed to go on forever, tanned, muscled, strong. She sighed. Edgar followed close behind him, carefully picking up clumps of grass, shaking the dirt off them then carrying them to a neat pile at the edge of the garden. The old man smiled and laughed and seemed to be talking nonstop. Scooter rooted his nose through the fresh earth, his white-tipped tail wagging furiously.

Janet shivered, unable to tear her eyes away from the scene, fascinated by the rippling muscles beneath the T-shirt. She could almost smell the fresh earth. She'd always wanted a garden and still did, but darned if she saw how she would have time to garden in the face of all the endless turmoil. Or in the proximity of those gorgeous legs. Of course, knowing her green thumb, or the lack thereof, everything would die before it got far enough along to worry about.

She finally went to shower and face whatever new crisis was bound to be afoot in the kitchen.

Fortunately the kitchen was quiet. No one but Lucas would be up at this ungodly hour. Even Clarence was passed out—or dead, she could never tell which—in his Dutch oven. She brewed coffee and sat down to enjoy it in the peace and quiet. Which didn't last long. She heard loud voices headed for the kitchen.

"Mrs. Heunfield, Verla's forgetful sometimes, but she didn't mean anything by it." Bea's voice floated toward the kitchen. Janet poured more coffee and waited for the latest disaster to reach her.

"Mrs. McNair, I'm sure I understand as well as anyone, but really. I didn't realize I was coming to a nursing home. I thought you were running a bed and breakfast. I certainly seem to be paying for that."

"I'm sorry," Verla put in. "I was just trying to fix it. It was so pretty, but the lady missed some stitches in the middle. I wanted to fix it for her."

The three women steamed into the kitchen, Bea flushed, Mrs. Heunfield indignant, Verla clutching something the size of a table cloth, which might have started out as a snowflake.

Bea rushed to Janet. "Oh dear, I'm so glad you're here. We seem to have a bit of a problem. Perhaps you can straighten it out."

Janet smiled sweetly. "How about a nice cup of coffee for everyone, then we'll sort this thing out." She got everyone seated with coffee in front of them. "Now what's wrong?" she asked, although she had a good idea of what the problem was.

"This—this person," Mrs. Heunfield started, "was making off with my snowflakes."

"I was not!" Verla announced. "I wanted to help. I can do nice stitches. I can fix it." The woman looked at Bea, her lips quivering. "I'm all right, Bea. Really I am."

Bea patted Verla's arm. "I know...."

"I've never in my life been accosted in a bed and breakfast," the matron cried.

"Ladies, ladies," Janet called over the shrill voices.

"You see, my dear, Mrs. Heunfield was showing me her snowflakes and we were out in the hall, and poor Verla—"

"I know, Bea. Verla has just explained. She wanted to help Mrs. Heunfield with a mistake. Obviously Mrs. Heunfield didn't want help. I'll just go get Verla's afghan and she can work on it." Janet poured more coffee and wanted to glare at the guest. "Now, everybody wait here and be calm. I'll be right back. Okay?"

"Young woman, I don't know what kind of place you're running here, but—"

"Just think about the old proverb—or whatever it is—Mrs. Heunfield. 'There but for the Grace of God go I'? I'll be right back."

She hurried upstairs and dug around in Verla's room and finally found the afghan jammed under the dresser. She lugged it back to the kitchen. "Here you go, Verla. I can't wait till you finish this. It's—just beautiful."

Verla grabbed the afghan and held it close to her. "I'm sorry, Janet. I wasn't trying to steal anything. I wasn't having a spell."

Janet stroked the woman's cheek. "I know you weren't. And it would have been okay, even if you had been. It takes time to get all that medicine out of your system. But you're getting better every day. That's what you have to remember. Okay? Now why don't you go see if Inez is awake. Maybe cheer her up. She wasn't feeling too good last night." Verla smiled and hurried off to help her friend. Janet turned to the guest. "Now, Mrs. Heunfield, everything is fine isn't it?" she said through clenched teeth.

"Well...I still don't know why you put up with her."

Janet flushed with anger. "She's old, her family has, for all practical purposes, cast her out, the nursing home she was in pumped her full of tranquilizers and that's why she forgets things. It scares her, and she panics and does things sometimes, trying to allay that scariness. But she was *not* having a spell. She was trying to help you."

"Well..."

"If we live long enough, Mrs. Heunfield, we all have some memory loss," she said quietly. She looked at the woman's face and saw fear and offense. "I'm sorry, I didn't mean to get on my soapbox, but...I'm sorry. Breakfast will be ready shortly." She busied herself with muffins, ashamed that she had lost her temper with the woman. She seemed to lose her temper a lot these days.

Bea smoothed her hair. "You haven't a thing to worry about, Mrs. Heunfield. We want all our guests to be happy." She smiled at her ruffled guest. "Of course, we certainly don't expect you to pay when there is any unpleasantness. Today is on us."

Janet almost dropped the coffee pot. "Bea!"

Mrs. Heunfield relaxed visibly. "Well, in that case."

Janet knew there would be some kind of unpleasantness each day unless she squelched it in the bud—now. "Naturally you realize there's a limit of one unpleasantness per stay, Mrs. Heunfield," she said sweetly.

"Humph."

The woman sailed out of the kitchen and Janet glared at Bea. "Bea, we agreed to discuss these things anytime there was a question about rates. Remember?"

"Oh, but she was so upset."

"I imagine she's been upset for years."

When she finished serving Mrs. Heunfield and Pete Bradley in the dining room and Bea, Inez and Verla in the kitchen, she fixed a tray of muffins and coffee and went to the backyard. She didn't particularly want to see Lucas, but she couldn't stand the kitchen a moment longer. She might flog Mrs. Heunfield to death with a scone.

She set her tray on the picnic table and made motions in Lucas's direction. She finally had to go stand in front of the tiller and wave her arms before he noticed her. He killed the engine and the quiet spring morning descended on them. She waved at the table. "I brought coffee and stuff." She turned. He touched her arm.

"What's wrong?"

"Nothing."

"I'd like to think that you're giving me such good service because you love me, but it's more likely you're out here because you can't stand it in there anymore." He gestured toward the house.

Janet sputtered at length before she could get any words out. "Look, do you want to analyze me or eat the muffins?" she finally said more sharply than she'd intended. Her nerves were a mess.

"Come on, Edgar." He led Edgar to the table and Janet fixed his coffee and muffin.

"Luke and me are plantin' us a fine garden, Miz Janet."

Janet looked up. Edgar's eyes looked so clear this morning. Maybe the garden would keep him out of the artist's hair. Now if she could get Verla involved with something else. She'd talked to the doctor, but he'd told her no more than she already knew—that only time, exercise and a good diet would bring Verla back. And that they could expect relapses from time to time. The awful thing was she'd been trying to help when that old harridan accused her of stealing. "I'm glad, Edgar."

Scooter flopped on the ground, panting. His nose was coated with a layer of fresh earth.

Lucas came back from washing at the outside tap. Drops of water glistened in his hair and on his face. He ate and drank in silence, watching Janet.

Edgar gulped the last of his coffee. "Got to get back to it, Luke. Those clumps get harder to find when they're dry."

"Be with you in a minute, Edgar." Lucas poured more coffee. "Now, are you going to tell me what happened this morning?"

"Nothing of any importance. Just a little altercation with Verla and a guest over a snowflake, which nobody in their right mind would want anyway."

He leaned back in his chair and rubbed the stubble on his chin. "Janet, you know it isn't working, don't you?"

"I don't know any such thing. We just happened to get a couple of jerks for guests. They won't all be like that."

His hand covered hers. "I think you're wrong. People don't like to be around any kind of disability—it reminds them of their own mortality. Look, I see it every day." He tossed Scooter a bit of muffin.

"I don't believe that." She didn't want to believe it, at any rate. She had spent the past few years mostly in the company of other nurses, and she just hadn't been exposed to the sort of thing he was talking about.

"Janet, people are coming here to relax, get away from their problems. They don't want to be reminded at every turn that someday they'll get old. It scares the hell out of most people. They're very good at ignoring it and hoping it will go away."

She felt his warm, strong hand on hers and wondered how gracefully he would age. She had a feeling he would still be going to the office when he was a hundred. "It won't be a problem forever. They're both so much better. You didn't see them when they first got here."

"I'm sure they're better, but you don't know if Edgar will ever regain all his memory permanently. And what if Verla has permanent damage?"

"He will, and she doesn't. I just know. Because the doctors say. Because—because it's going to work out."

He smiled. "You just go right on thinking that. You also go right on thinking about the effects these little altercations have on Mom."

"That's dirty pool. I—"

He stood up before she could respond further. "What you need is a day of good hard work in the garden. Clean dirt, hot sun, bugs—all that good stuff. Go put on some old clothes and get to it."

She smiled in spite of herself and took the tray back to the kitchen. She had no intention of spending the day with him—even with Edgar as a chaperone. Five minutes in the kitchen with Verla, Bea and Inez, however, changed her mind. "I'm going to the garden," she announced. "Inez, you're in charge of Clarence. Verla, you're in charge of afghans. Bea, you're in charge of everything else." She went to change into ragged cutoffs and an old Beatles T-shirt.

She was totally unprepared for the appreciative stare Lucas cast at her legs. After all, he'd seen them once. She wished she'd worn jeans. "What do you want me to do?"

"That's a leading question, but I assume you're referring to the garden."

She ignored his quirky grin and tried to ignore his skimpy shorts. "I thought that's why you invited me out here." She noticed strings stretched over the fresh soil he had tilled and raked.

"You can plant the onions." He pulled a shriveled wad of something that looked like weeds out of a sack and dropped to his knees beside the first string. "All you have to do is stick these in the ground about so deep." He made a hole in the dirt with his finger, shoved a scrawny plant in and firmed the soil around it with his hand. "About two inches apart."

Janet crouched down across the string from him, their knees almost touching, and tried her best to ignore his smell. She'd never thought about combining the smells of dirt, clean sweat and male, but it was a deadly combination. She breathed deeply. "You mean to tell me these ratty little things are going to make onions?"

His face was inches from hers. "Yes. In a few weeks, they'll be bright green and ready to eat. The ones you don't use for green onions will mature into big onions. Just like you buy in the store."

"Really?" She had never imagined the study of onions could be so fascinating. She poked her finger in the dirt and stuck an onion in, then covered it. The damp soil smelled of leaf mold and forest humus. The sun warmed her back.

"If you want long, green onions, you plant them a little deeper. If you want mature bulbs, you plant them a little shallower."

"I never knew that."

He stuck another onion in the ground. "It's a big secret."

Janet was rapidly forgetting the trials of the morning as her enthusiasm began to take hold. "What else are we going to have? Can we have radishes in the next row?"

"Radishes and lettuce."

"Can't we have a whole row of radishes?"

He sat back on his feet and laughed. "Do you have any idea how many radishes you get from twenty feet of row?"

"I like radishes." She poked onions in the ground and carefully firmed them.

"But they all come on at once when you plant them at once."

"They do?"

"They do. Since you were in such a swivet yesterday and didn't tell me what you wanted, I went to town last night and bought a little of everything. Corn, beans, tomato and pepper plants. And your favorite." He leaned close. "Butternut squash."

"You didn't," she said, waiting for the flush to start.

"I did. Now, plant your onions while I finish tilling. If we're lucky—and you don't have any more crises—we'll get it all in today."

She planted onions, scolding Scooter occasionally for rooting in her neat row—and studiously ignored the bare legs that swept by her with every pass of the tiller. And wondered what was going on beneath that sweaty shock of dark curly hair. Regardless of what he said, she knew Lucas still planned to move Bea sooner or later. He'd quit ranting and raving about how it wasn't going to work. He was carefully pointing out little things to her, instead. Throwing out doubts. And she was catching every one of them—and Lucas knew it—although she wasn't just about to admit it to him. Which made his job ever so much easier. All he had to do was hang around and be charming, wait for her to make the decision to give up. Which would put the black hat on her and the white hat on him, at least in Bea's eyes. She would have to figure out some way to solve the temporary problem of interaction between guests and the old folks. There had to be a way. She couldn't look Bea in the eye and tell her they had to close down. He was using her to get his way, and it wasn't fair. She jabbed onions into the soft ground. Oh, it was all his fault. He was the one sowing doubts. She had to ignore them. Which was getting more difficult every day.

She jumped at the feel of a hand on her head. "Lunchtime," Lucas said. He reached out to pull her up and she let him, regretting it when the warm feeling rushed up her arm.

"Come along, everyone," Bea called from the table beneath the oak tree. "It's a cold lunch, I'm afraid. I've been helping Verla with a snowflake.

Orange. But at least maybe she'll forget the afghan. It's quite large enough to carpet a room.''

Janet shuddered at the thought of giant orange snowflakes hanging all over the house, and brushed the dirt off, then followed Lucas to the spigot and washed her face and hands. "I can't believe the morning's gone."

He grinned and flipped a drop of water at her. "Time flies when you're havin' fun."

"More country wisdom?" She wanted to put her head under the spigot and cool off but decided against it. She might drown herself.

"Can't beat it. You know, don't you, that this garden's going to be a lot of work." He draped an arm over her shoulder as they walked toward the table.

"I know. But it's fun." His arm seemed so right, so natural, so nice, so warm. While he was so confident, so cool, so...unaffected.

"You may not think so come July."

"I can handle it." And the beds and the cleaning and the fussing and everything else. "No problem."

"I think Edgar can help, but he'll have to be supervised for a while." They sat down and began to eat. "You know, come to think of it, he hasn't mentioned trains all morning."

Janet felt a surge of hope. "I think it's because he has a purpose again. Maybe he's turned the corner."

Bea patted Lucas's hand. "I'm sorry lunch is not hot, dear."

"Mother, I haven't eaten hot lunches since I left home. I usually grab a sandwich. It's fine."

"Lucas, you have to eat a nice, hot lunch. Oh, I knew you weren't eating right."

"I'm eating fine, Mom. Just fine." He finished a sandwich and started another. "I'm going to take Edgar fishing this afternoon after we finish the garden. You want to go, Janet?"

She shook her head, unable to speak around the large bite of sandwich she'd just taken. She shifted for the third time so that her bare knees wouldn't touch his bare knees.

"Are there ants in your...uh, chair?" he asked solicitously, his eyes dancing with laughter.

"I think they're under the table," she muttered.

"Ants? Isn't it too early?" Bea searched the table for any evidence of the enemy.

Lucas laughed and bumped her with his knee, daring her to squirm again. "Maybe we can take the boat out after supper. To continue your phobia antiphobia training."

Janet smiled and moved her leg, sure that all she would want to do after supper was fall into bed. "We'll see. I have a lot to do."

"Of course she'll go, dear. I'll clean up tonight." Bea patted Janet's hand. "After all, we can't have you falling out of a boat and drowning just because you were too tired for your lesson."

"Bea, if I never get into a boat, the likelihood of that happening is very remote."

"But one never knows when one might need to travel by boat."

"Right." Janet carried the tray back to the kitchen and returned to her garden. She scattered tiny lettuce seeds, and Lucas carefully covered them behind her. She planted radish seed—more than he wanted—and dug neat holes for the pepper and tomato plants. Edgar fussed over every little blade of grass and chattered away about gardens and tools—and no trains. She was pleased.

After they'd watered everything, she stood back and admired it. "It's beautiful."

Lucas wiped his face with a towel Bea had brought. "It doesn't look like much now, but give it a month." He looked at her with a frown.

"A month." She knew what he was thinking. That neither of them would be here in a month. She felt a sharp stab to think that in a month's time he would be long gone, back to his life in the city. And where would she be? The thought that she very much wanted him to stay hit her with the force of a lightning bolt. Regardless of what happened with Bea, with her, she wanted him here. He belonged here on his land. She flushed.

"Janet, I didn't mean—"

"Well, when will the weeds appear?" she said brightly, turning away.

He studied her a moment longer then shrugged. "Tomorrow, probably. They grow much faster than the vegetables. Sure you don't want a fishing lesson?" He walked behind her, and once again she was all too aware of his earthy smell.

"No thanks. Maybe some other time." She wanted to get away from him, try to figure out when she'd begun to fall so hopelessly in love with a man she couldn't possibly hope to have. He would never come back, and she had no desire to return to Little Rock. She loved it here and thought she would stay in the area, even if Bea no longer needed her.

"Okay. Let's go, Edgar," Lucas said, stopping.

"Hey, Luke—you think we'll find any crappie? It's about time for them to be running, if I recall."

"We'll do our best, buddy."

Janet showered and dressed then sat by the window to brush her hair. The little boat sat motionless on the mirrored lake, not far from the dock. Edgar smiled as Lucas did something with his line then helped him cast toward the island. She so hoped Edgar would recover completely. He would be a real asset as a grounds keeper, and he would be around people who cared. Edgar needed people. She squinted and could just barely see the little red corks bobbing on the quiet water. Lucas sat in quiet profile, smiling and saying something occasionally.

Janet felt an ache well up. It was more than the dull ache she'd carefully buried in the months since Jack left. This was a piercing ache for love and closeness and a gentle man's touch. But not this man. She had no doubt he would be more than willing to fix her ache, use that ache to convince her to shut down Crow's Rest. But he would leave at month's end, and eventually he would take Bea with him. If not this month, then another month. And she would be left with an ache worse than any she'd known.

CHAPTER SEVEN

JANET STARTED to get up, groaned and fell back on the bed, her muscles refusing to cooperate. She considered going back to sleep then thought better of it. She didn't want to give Lucas the satisfaction of knowing her legs wouldn't work after a little gardening. After much stretching and pulling she managed to get to the shower. She couldn't believe she could be so sore from that little bit of work, then she decided it was probably not the gardening at all but the boat ride after supper—thirty minutes with all her muscles fully tensed.

She stood under the hot water and thought about the boat ride. Lucas had seemed more relaxed than she'd ever seen him. They'd talked—about everything and nothing—and laughed, and then on the way back he'd become strangely silent. She didn't think she'd said anything to anger him, and he hadn't really seemed angry, just pulled back into himself. She dried herself and dressed, thinking she would never understand him. Not, of course, that she wanted to, still . . .

When she wobbled into the kitchen, flexing her sore legs, Lucas was mixing muffins. "Well, how are you this morning?"

She wasn't in the mood for bright and chipper this morning. "I should have known you'd be a gourmet cook, too," she muttered.

"What was that?"

"I'm just fine. Couldn't be better."

A grin tugged at his mouth. "Why are you walking funny then?"

"I'm not walking funny." She quit walking funny, and the muscles in her legs screamed their objections.

"It's from being down on your knees so much. Moving up and down is hard on the quads." He expertly filled the muffin tins and popped them in the oven.

She poured coffee. "My quads are just fine."

He leaned against the counter, sipped at his coffee and lifted his leg to nudge her thigh with a bare foot. "I could rub them, loosen them up a little."

"No, thank you." She imagined those strong hands running up and down her thighs. Then she forced herself to remember that he was charming her into the role of being the heavy with Bea. It didn't help as it should have.

He stretched his arms above his head. "I'm a little stiff this morning, myself. That tiller is a real bear."

She smiled sweetly. "Good. I'm glad to hear it. Where's Bea?"

He shrugged. "She's not up yet."

"Not up yet?" Worry nibbled at Janet. Bea was always up at this hour. Of course, Lucas couldn't possibly know that. "You haven't checked on her?"

"No, why?" He frowned. "I just assumed she was sleeping in."

"It's probably nothing. I'll just go check."

He caught her arm. "She hasn't had any trouble, has she?"

"No." Just as she got up to go check, Bea bustled into the kitchen.

"Oh, dear, I seem to have overslept. My, you two are looking serious this morning."

Janet unobtrusively scrutinized the woman's face and saw no signs of flushing or pain. "Are you all right, Bea?"

"Why, of course I am, dear. All the excitement about the garden made me a little tired. It will be so nice to have fresh vegetables again. Not like those nasty things one buys at the store. Lucas, dear, you didn't have to make the muffins." She winked at Janet. "He's wonderful in the kitchen."

The first crisis of the day averted, Janet slumped back in her chair and drank coffee. "So I see."

Lucas poured more coffee and added milk. "I sure wish we still had Ophelia, Mom. Coffee hasn't been the same since."

"Who's Ophelia?" Janet asked then decided she probably didn't want to know. It was probably a friend of Clarence's.

Bea sighed. "She was our last milk cow. A beautiful little Jersey. I do miss her."

Lucas bent over to whisper in Janet's ear. "She's been gone for fifteen years." He turned to Bea. "Do the MacFarlands still have that dairy across the lake?"

"They have a few cows left, but Horace is quite old now. Lucas, why don't you go see them. I'm sure Hattie would give you some cream."

"I might just do that."

Janet looked at Lucas sideways. "I suppose you used to milk the cow." She found the fact that he could do anything and everything disgusting this morning.

"Champion milker. Did you ever milk a cow?"

"There aren't many cows in Little Rock."

"Well, it's a nice experience. Cold mornings, run to the barn and nestle your face against a warm flank." He stared out the kitchen window, a strange, faraway look on his face. "Warm, steamy milk for the cats, all the butter you want and cream so thick you can stand a spoon up in it."

"Cholesterol City," Janet quipped.

"Ah, but what a way to go." He snapped his attention back to the kitchen. "Maybe when we expand this place, we'll have a cow. Think of the pastries all that butter would make. Devonshire cream for high tea."

Bea brightened immediately. "Lucas, are we going to expand?" She took the muffins from the oven and set them on the table, nodding all the while at Janet. "You see, I told you he'd come around. I knew he'd see things our way."

Janet glared at Lucas. Darn him anyway, leading her on like that. "That's what worries me. Bea, as much as I'd love the experience of milking a cow, I don't think we can handle it. I'm sure there are all sorts of laws about raw milk."

Bea chortled. "Oh, you're getting as bad as Lucas about details."

Lucas's dark eyes twinkled. "She's right, Mom. A cow is too much work. Janet's got more than she can say grace over now."

"It has nothing to do with work. It has to do with the Health Department." She drank coffee and glared at him. "There's hardly any work at all to this place." At that moment Inez lumbered into the kitchen, looking pale and enormous.

Bea helped her to a chair. "You look a little peaked this morning, dear. Are you all right?"

The girl nodded.

"When is she due?" Lucas asked.

"Any day," Janet replied tiredly.

"Well, shouldn't you be doing something?" He shifted nervously in his chair. Inez burst into tears.

Janet sighed and poured more coffee. The closer Inez came to her delivery time, the more she tended toward crying jags. Janet had tried to calm the girl's fears by carefully explaining the entire procedure, but it hadn't helped. "What would you suggest we do? Keep the water boiling? The baby will come when it's good and ready. There will be plenty of time to do something when she starts labor." Inez sobbed louder. "Inez, take deep breaths. We're going to get you through this just fine. Okay?"

Clarence bestirred himself long enough to cross the kitchen and jump up beside the pan of muffins. Janet snatched him away and gave him a muffin on the floor. "If we did get a milk cow, do you think we could relocate Clarence to the barn? Permanently?"

Before anyone could answer, they heard the front door slam. "Are we due for guests, Janet?" Bea smoothed her hair.

"Not till this afternoon."

"Where is she?" someone yelled from the front of the house. Inez burst into a new round of tears.

Bea frowned. "Oh dear, it's her mother." She waved frantically toward Inez.

Janet thought seriously about drowning herself in hot coffee. "That's just what we need to start the day." At that moment a woman burst into the kitchen. She was large, with mousy brown hair and a good deal of mascara.

"There you are." She brandished a sheaf of papers at her daughter. "Sign these. It's all arranged. Some nice couple the lawyer found. They'll pay the doctor bills."

Bea fussed with her hair. "Would you like some coffee, Alma?"

"I didn't come for coffee, Bea. I came to get this stubborn child's signature on these papers. Besides, I'm not speaking to you. You're harboring a fugitive."

Bea grew even more flustered. "Alma, if you remember, you're the one who threw Inez out of the house. Now I won't have you upsetting the child."

"You think *I* haven't been upset all these months? Her shamin' me like this? Now I want these papers signed."

Janet watched the exchange, her anger growing by the minute at the sight of the person who had filled Inez's head with all her ridiculous old wives' tales.

"Mrs. Keyes, Inez is in my care and I won't have you upsetting her like this. Just leave the papers. If Inez wants to sign them, she can do it later."

The woman stared at Janet. "And just who are you?"

"She's a nurse, Alma. An RN," Bea announced as if that gave Janet all the authority in the world.

"And I suppose you're trying to talk her out of giving the kid up, just like Bea is?"

Janet bristled and felt herself flush. "No one is trying to talk her into or out of anything. It's Inez's decision."

"She hasn't got sense enough to make a decision."

Janet exploded. She stood up and waved a rigid finger in the woman's face. "You talk about sense? After all the drivel you've filled her head with? Let me tell you about sense, you—you . . . twit!"

A hand touched Janet's arm and gently pushed her aside. Lucas stood glaring down at the woman. "Do I take it that you and your attorney have arranged to *sell* Inez's infant?"

"Who—you must be little Lucas. We're not selling anything. We just made arrangements. I have the right. She's not eighteen yet."

He snatched the papers out of the woman's hands. "As Inez's attorney, I will take a look at these papers and be in touch. But I can tell you right now that she *does* have the right to keep her child if she wishes."

"She can't." But the woman sounded less sure than before.

"Oh, but she can. Now I think you'd better leave. You're upsetting my mother."

The woman sputtered and threatened a moment longer, then stomped out.

Inez's sobbing dwindled away. "I don't know what I'd do without you all. I—I'm sorry, I didn't want her to come here and make a scene. I thought she'd given up. Thank you for everything." She burst into a fresh round of tears. "Why can't I do anything without bawling?"

Janet squeezed her hand. "It's the pregnancy, Inez. Some women just have a rough time. I'll get you some milk."

Bea reached up to kiss Lucas. "You were just wonderful, dear. Sometimes that woman quite unhinges me."

Janet knelt beside Inez, still in shock over Lucas's intervening for Inez. He'd been impressive, to say the least. "Inez, no one is going to take your baby unless you decide. Okay? Now quit crying. It's not good for you. She handed her the glass of milk and urged her to drink. Then she turned to look at Lucas. He was dark with anger, his eyes flashing black. She realized at that moment just what a formidable adversary he could be.

"I'm going to town for a while. Is there anything you want me to pick up?"

Bea handed him a grocery list. "Would you mind?"

"Not at all," he said stiffly.

Janet watched him stalk out of the house and heard his car peel out of the driveway. She was tickled to death that he'd agreed—more or less—to help Inez, but she had a feeling that somewhere down the line, she would have to pay for the help. She wasn't even sure what she meant by that; she just had a feeling.

She turned back to Inez. "Remember how I told you to breathe? Let's try it. Deep breaths." She breathed in unison with the girl until Inez's pulse rate dropped and her redness faded. "Good."

"I do want to keep her."

Janet smiled. "A girl, huh? I hope so. Little girls are nice. All the pretty lace and ruffles. You just hang on to those thoughts, Inez. Don't pay any attention to anyone else."

"I think I'll go check on Verla." The girl smiled. "You know, she's doing a lot better. We crocheted all yesterday afternoon and she was fine. I think she's going to be okay."

Janet hugged Inez. "Thanks in large part to you, Inez. You've done wonders with her." The girl blushed and headed toward the sitting room.

Janet spent the rest of the day cooking and cleaning. And listening for Lucas's car. She found, much to her dismay, that she missed him. He was such a strange mixture. Tender, sensitive, wonderful, even when he was angry. She scrubbed at a table with wax, uneasy with such thoughts, but she knew Crow's Rest would seem empty when he left. Well, maybe that emptiness would make it easier for her to leave, too, when the time came.

She had totally refused to deal with her feelings for him, but she knew, in the afternoon quietness of the old farm house, that she could love him. Knew, really, that she already did, although she pushed that thought aside quickly. He'd given her no reason to believe he felt anything toward her. Oh, he'd teased, but it was the kind of teasing that came naturally to handsome men. He was just being charming and giving her the time and space she needed to come to her own conclusion about Crow's Rest—giving her enough rope to hang herself. She knew—and realized he knew—that if he ranted and raved, she would defend the operation to the death. Oh, he was playing her perfectly, and she resented him for it, resented him for understanding her so completely. Resented him for making her love him.

By mid-afternoon, she had taken a long walk, cleaned two closets and led her little class through all the aerobic exercises she knew. And still she felt frustrated and antsy and in danger.

When he returned late in the afternoon, he was his usual teasing, confident, smug self. He unloaded the groceries and refused to tell them anything about where he'd been or what had happened. All he would say was that things were under control as far as Inez was concerned. They sat down to tea as if nothing had ever happened. Janet was feeling better, since there had been no major disasters during the day. Pete Bradley had disappeared for the day, Mrs. Heunfield had gone to Eureka Springs to see the Passion Play, the house was quiet. She relaxed—as much as she ever relaxed in the presence of Lucas—and sipped tea, which she still hated.

Lucas set down his tea cup. "Go change into your jeans, Janet. I have a surprise for you."

She immediately tensed. "What kind of surprise?" she asked suspiciously. He'd probably decided she was ready for swimming or waterskiing.

"Well now, it wouldn't be a surprise if I told you, would it?"

"I don't like surprises." She was not going to put herself in any more situations designed to get her in deeper than she already was. Now that he was back, she wished he would go away again.

Bea reached over and patted her knee. "Of course you do, dear."

Lucas reached over and patted the other knee. Janet felt warm all over, but she insisted, "I have things to do."

He kept patting. "You're a stick-in-the-mud. We're going to the MacFarlands to get cream. Do-it-yourself cream."

"Do-it-yourself cream?" Every time his hand tapped her knee, it felt like a jolt from a hot wire.

"I went to see Horace today. When I told him we were thinking about getting a cow, he said to come over and try his."

"You're kidding." Janet stood up to get away from his hand.

"Oh, Lucas, are you thinking about getting another Ophelia?" Bea looked enraptured at the thought.

"All our cows were named Ophelia. Mom said it was easier that way. You know, when they passed on to the big cow pasture in the sky."

Janet's eyes grew wide. "I repeat my original comment. You're kidding."

"Would I kid you about a thing like that?"

"You mean you just try out a cow, like you would a used car? That sounds...tacky." She was certain he was pulling her leg. "Besides, I thought we decided against the cow." Somehow, she wasn't sure about liking the warm flank on cold mornings. Which made her think of other warm things on cold mornings, and she reddened a little.

"Well, I thought it would be fun to try my hand at milking after all these years." He touched Janet's cheek. "You're a little flushed. Is it too hot in here?" His eyes danced with laughter.

"It's the hot air you're pouring into the room." She brushed the hair off her fevered brow as she spoke.

"Run on and change, dear. You'll love Horace's cows. They're Jerseys."

Janet went to change, full of misgivings. There was more to this cow business than met the eye—of that she was sure. But there wasn't really any nice way to get out of it. She refused to admit that the excitement she felt was at the thought of going somewhere—any-where—with Lucas. After all, she should be perfectly safe in the presence of Horace and a Jersey cow.

She sat as far to her side of the car as she could, with the window wide open. Horace and the cow might be safer than getting *to* Horace and the cow. Being trapped in the car with Lucas was worse than being trapped in the kitchen by far. She finally decided to tax him with his promises to Bea. A good argument might make her forget she was trapped. "Lucas, I don't think it's fair for you to lead Bea down the garden path, making her think we're going to expand and all that nonsense.''

He was silent for several minutes. ''Are you sure it's nonsense?''

''Well, of course it's nonsense. Where would she get the money?'' What was he talking about now?

''It's not a bad idea. The location is right.''

''And I suppose you're going to run the place?''

He grinned. ''I don't *do* hotels. I do lawyering.''

''I don't know what you have in mind, but I do know you shouldn't raise false hopes.'' When he didn't respond, she continued. ''I also know you're trying to make me the heavy in the whole thing. You're trying your best to point out in various and sundry ways how much work the place is, how upset Bea gets, how guests and old folks don't mix, so I'll be the one to finally tell her it wasn't a good idea.'' There, she'd got it out.

''Is that what you think?'' He gave her a questioning sideways glance.

''Well, isn't that what you're doing?'' But her voice lacked conviction.

''And are you trying to convince me you don't have any doubts? I don't believe that for a minute. Not after the kind of week you've had.''

''Well, things are beginning to settle down. Edgar has been clear as a bell since we started the garden, and Verla hasn't had a serious lapse in ages.''

He was silent for a long moment. ''You think I'm a real jerk, don't you?'' His voice was soft, yet the tone was hard as steel.

"No. I think...I don't know what to think." She'd been so sure of his motives, now she wasn't sure about anything.

"Well, rest assured I don't unload the dirty work on other people. If I decide to close the place down, *I'll* do it!"

She winced at the anger in his voice. Maybe he wasn't using her to do the deed, but he seemed awfully sure of himself when it came to running other people's lives, which raised her own anger. "Just like that? Doesn't Bea have anything to say about it?"

"Up to a point, Janet. Only up to a point. We're here." He pulled the car into a gravel drive.

She knew the discussion was over, and she was left worrying about that mysterious point at which he would take action.

A few minutes later she and Lucas and a grizzled man stood at the door of a stall in a tidy barn, looking at a golden-brown cow with the biggest, brownest eyes Janet had ever seen.

"I thought you might try Katy here, Luke. She'll milk from both sides. And she's gentle as a lamb."

Lucas ran his hand over the cow as the old man dumped feed in a trough. His anger seemed to be a thing of the past. "Usually you milk from the right side only," he explained. "Some cows will let two people milk them, one on each side."

"She's beautiful." Janet touched the slick hide as Lucas squatted with the bucket. The cow's thick tail swatted her leg.

"You can have the stool." He pointed to something that looked like two boards made into a T.

"That's a stool?" She picked it up but couldn't imagine how anyone could possibly sit on it. "It doesn't have any legs."

"It's a milking stool used in these parts. It requires a little balance." He wiped the cow's udder with a wet cloth. "Maybe you better forget the stool."

She squatted beside him and watched him massage the udder. It was close in the barn, and the cow smelled warm and clean. She stroked the cow's flank as Lucas showed her what to do.

"The trick is to trap the milk in the teat with the thumb and index finger—like so—then squeeze it out with the other fingers." A stream of bright white milk hit the side of the bucket, then another. "Here, try it."

She grasped the teat and squeezed. Nothing happened. She tried again. Nothing. Suddenly a cat appeared and rubbed against her back. "Hi, kitty."

"Lean back a minute."

Janet watched in amazement as Lucas directed a stream of milk toward the cat who sat up on its haunches and caught every drop. Janet clapped her hands in delight. "I don't believe that. How does he do it?"

Lucas smiled and gave the cat another squirt. "I can't believe I can still do that after all these years. Probably because Horace has them so well trained. Ready to try again?" His hand covered hers. "It's a rhythm. Squeeze with the thumb and finger, then come down with the other fingers."

Janet still chuckled over the cat. She had seen a moment of real delight in Lucas. Not the smug, teasing laughter she had grown accustomed to, but real joy, real laughter. That, combined with the warmth of the barn and his closeness made her head swim. She concentrated on the milking and got a drop, then a tiny stream.

"Okay. Just keep at it. I'll take the other side." He walked around the cow and began to milk.

As Janet struggled with the technique, the bucket filled up with warm, foamy milk, the sound of the milk hitting the bucket changing as the level rose. Occasionally Lucas would squirt milk toward the cat, which had moved to his side of the cow. Janet laughed heartily each time. She finally began to get a respectable squirt of milk with each squeeze. "Aren't we hurting her?"

He laughed. "No. She likes to be milked. If you don't milk them, it becomes very painful."

"Oh." Janet concentrated on the rhythm and began to get a nice, small stream. Nothing like Lucas's, but she thought it was quite respectable. She ignored the fact that her hands touched his each time she squeezed. She also tried to ignore the fact that her hands were beginning to cramp. She felt the cow move and looked up to see that Katy had finished her feed and turned her head to stare at Janet with those big beautiful eyes. "Hi, Katy. Sorry this is taking forever," she whispered, "but I don't know what I'm doing." She heard a chuckle from the other side of the cow.

Lucas appeared beside her and squatted to finish what she had started. The muscles in his arms rippled to the rhythm of the milking. His gentleness made her feel warm and tingly all over. She jumped in relief when Horace came back in, a brimming bucket of milk in each hand.

"See you ain't lost your touch, Luke."

"Ah, she's a fine cow, Horace. Easy milker." He picked up the bucket and rubbed the cow on the knot between her horns, a faraway look in his eyes.

"How'd you do, missy?" He looked Janet up and down.

"Not too good, I'm afraid."

"Well, it takes a while to get the hang of it. Back in my prime the missus and me milked eighteen head a day."

Janet stared in awe. "All by yourselves? You must have been able to crush walnuts in your hands," she said, rubbing her cramped hands.

"Yes, ma'am. Didn't have no milkin' machines in those days, wouldn't have used them if we had. I've always believed a cow likes the touch of a warm hand to do her best."

They started toward the house. "Bring that on in, Luke. The missus'll strain her up for you."

"I appreciate it, Horace. What do I owe you?"

"Not a thing, boy. Anytime you want to milk, you just come right on over. My old hands ain't what they used to be and I'm glad for the help. If'n you want Katy, you just let me know. She's a corker. She'll give you a calf a year and all the milk and butter and such as you could want."

"I'll let you know, Horace. Thanks."

A few minutes later they were headed home with a gallon of fresh milk on the seat between them. Janet was silent, wondering why Lucas had brought her. She didn't think it had anything to do with milk or cows. Somehow, she thought it had to do with...roots. Which was strange, because she didn't think Lucas was the least bit interested in his roots. Now that they were away from the cow, he seemed almost angry that they'd come. He was strangely silent all the way home and she wondered for the umpteenth time what was going on in that head of his.

She worried endlessly about the conversation they'd had on the way to the MacFarlands. If he wasn't using her to convince Bea they had a tiger by the tail, what on earth was he doing? It was almost as if he were trying out for size all the things he remembered. As if he were testing to see if one could really go home. Which made even less sense to her than anything she'd thought of so far. The trip had been fun, too much fun. She renewed her resolve to stay away from him, stay away from the temptation to love him, to need him.

CHAPTER EIGHT

WHEN JANET TOOK her first cup of coffee and wandered into the yard a couple of mornings later, she was surprised to find Edgar working alone in the garden with a hoe. "Edgar, is there anything to hoe yet?" She walked closer and couldn't see a thing until she bent close. A veritable carpet of tiny weeds had popped up virtually overnight. She was appalled yet fascinated with their vigor and enthusiasm. She began to imagine just how much work a garden might be.

"You bet, Miz Janet. Got to keep ahead of 'em. You wait till she really needs hoein', it's too late."

He carefully scraped the weeds away from what she assumed were the rows, although she wasn't sure. She kept hoping the onions would show some signs of life, but there they stood just as she had planted them. Only the peppers looked happy. "You really enjoy this, don't you Edgar?"

Edgar leaned on his hoe and smiled at her. "Yes ma'am I surely do. It makes me feel good."

She looked at him closely. His eyes were bright, no sign of the confusion that used to lie close to the surface. "That's nice, Edgar. That's really nice. When will something that we planted come up?"

"Few more days the lettuce and radishes'll be showin'. Few hot days the corn and beans'll pop up. Oh, it'll be a sight, it will."

"I know. I can't wait." She left him at his work and wandered back to the picnic table. She was excited, and was sure Edgar had passed some sort of milestone in his recovery. She was glad to see him happy. She was glad somebody was happy. She had almost come to the conclusion that what she needed to do was fade away quietly and leave Lucas to deal with Bea however he wanted. Yet she knew that was a coward's way out. At least the problem with Edgar was solved. Now if she could be as sure about Verla. As much as she hated to admit it, Lucas was likely right about people on vacation not wanting to be around people who had memory lapses. And even if the old folks recovered totally, there was still the problem of Lucas's concern for his mother's health.

Janet had wracked her brain worrying over what to do about Lucas. She was getting in deeper and deeper, knowing all the while it was a mistake but unable to help herself. She still wasn't totally convinced he wasn't using her to defeat Bea, but she was convinced she was going to end up the bad guy by default. As much as she believed in what Bea was doing, all it would take was one mild attack and Janet would be drowning in guilt and driving the woman to Little Rock herself. She loved Bea, and the thought of talking her out of her dream hurt. But the thought that Janet herself might be contributing to some disaster down the road hurt even more. She could walk away, but that wouldn't be fair to the older woman. Damn

Lucas, anyway. He was the one who was stirring up all these doubts.

And if that wasn't enough, now she teetered on the edge of falling head over heels in love with him. It had occurred to her sometime in the dark quiet of the night that her feelings were simply the feelings one got on the rebound and that if she succumbed to the infatuation, well, it would be out of her system and she could get on with her life. It occurred to her minutes later that if her rebound theory was wrong, the results would be disastrous for her.

She sighed, rather like a Victorian governess, she thought, and went to start her day's work. Perhaps she was destined to live a life of unrequited love, just like Heathcliffe. She shook herself angrily at the thought. "Quit being melodramatic and get to work," she muttered, and a robin cocked his head to listen.

Back in the house there was little to do. Mrs. Heunfield had called the night before and told them she was staying another day in Eureka Springs, the artist had gone off to visit a friend in Fayetteville, and the guest they were expecting had called to say she would be a day late. Lucas had disappeared on one of his mysterious trips to town. Scooter was in his chair, snoring and recovering from his work in the garden. Even Clarence refused to show any signs of life. Morning slowly dragged into afternoon.

"Bea, this place certainly is quiet this afternoon," she said. Bea was in the kitchen, trying a new recipe for something called meringue silkies.

"It's a bit of a relief, isn't it, dear?"

"Where's Verla?"

"She's in the sitting room, working on an enormous snowflake. I hope she doesn't insist on hanging it at Christmas. It will quite covering the entire living room. But she's as calm and cool as Verla ever was. Do you think—"

"Let's cross our fingers. Inez?"

"Resting. I think she's very near her time. I do hope her temperament improves somewhat after the baby is born."

"It will. She's awfully young, and she's terrified about the whole thing. No wonder, with that mother of hers."

"Oh, I almost forgot the good news, dear. Lucas spoke to some friend of his who has something to do with Social Security. Edgar has a new hearing for his disability next week. Lucas is sure it will be approved."

"Really?" She wondered why Lucas hadn't bothered to tell her. Probably because it substantiated her belief that he was still in the process of clearing out Crow's Rest. She was delighted for Edgar, since it would mean he was eligible for medical insurance and a host of other services, but she questioned Lucas's motivation. Which wasn't fair, she supposed.

"Yes, Lucas is very concerned about Edgar."

"What else has he been doing?" He was probably off arranging to put the furniture in storage.

"Well, he doesn't tell me everything, but he did tell me that he had squashed the plans of that young man who got Inez in trouble in the first place, then abandoned her, then started clamoring for *his* child. Lucas says he doesn't have a leg to stand on. I believe Lucas was quite stern with the young man. Of course, we all knew he was quite unsuitable right from the beginning."

"I'll just bet he was." So he was dabbling in a little law on his vacation and for some reason he didn't want her to know. "Bea, has Lucas talked to you any more about moving to Little Rock?"

The woman laughed. "Oh, he does prattle on about it from time to time, but I don't pay him the slightest mind."

"Hmm. How *would* you feel about...uh...you know, closing this place down?"

"What a silly idea, my dear. I love what we're doing. I know you're worried about some of the guests, but that will all sort itself out. Things do, you know."

"I know, but, well, it is isolated out here and even if we solve the problems with mixing old folks and guests, it's—"

"Janet, dear, problems have a way of solving themselves. Of course you're too young to know that yet, but trust me."

Before she could ask any more questions, Lucas appeared. Her heart beat a little faster at the sight of him.

"I'm starved."

"Oh dear. My meringue silkies aren't quite ready yet. At least I don't think they are." Bea gazed at the strange lumps of mainly egg white.

"Uh, I had more in mind meat and potatoes or something," he assured her after a look at the meringues.

Janet laughed in spite of herself at his look of concern over Bea's latest recipe. "You just don't have any class. Meringue silkies are the stuff high teas are made of."

"Janet's right, dear. I got the recipe out of a gourmet magazine."

Lucas ate a leftover muffin and looked properly chagrined. "I like meat and potatoes and corn bread and beans and all that good stuff." He looked at Janet. "And squash."

Janet made a face at him then flushed when he tweaked her nose. "I think I'll clean the closets this evening."

"I have a better idea," Lucas said, taking her arm. "Let's go to the island and have a picnic." He held up his hand to stop the protest he obviously knew was coming. "No excuses. No guests today, Edgar is busy in the garden and Verla seems to be trapped happily in her chair under a giant snowflake. Mom will pack us a basket, won't you, Mom?"

Bea immediately began bustling. "I think it's a wonderful idea. I have some ham, and let me see...." She buried her head in the refrigerator.

"It's time we took the boat out a little farther, since you're progressing so well in your lessons." His voice teased.

"Uh, I think I'll pass." Given her present state of confusion and...other feelings, she wasn't about to traipse off to an island with him.

He put an arm around her shoulders and pulled her close. "You really don't have any choice in the matter," he whispered. "You can come quietly, or I can carry you kicking and screaming.'' He smiled and gave her cheek a light peck.

''You wouldn't.'' She seemed to be drowning in his closeness.

''I would.''

She thought about struggling but knew it was useless, and as much as she hated to admit it, her heart just wasn't in it. She wanted to go, wanted to be with him, needed to test her new feelings. She sighed. One more resolution out the window. ''You would.''

''Right. Go change. You might try, oh, twenty pounds of clothes this time instead of forty.''

Janet growled at him and went to her room. She planned to use the time on the island to find out just what he'd been doing and what he had in mind for the future. And whatever it was, she would put a stop to it of course, unless he happened to be teetering on the same brink she was. Which was unlikely. No hanky-panky on the island for her, regardless of what he had in mind. So why was her heart pounding with excitement about going?

SHE MADE THE TRIP to the island clutching only the seat, not the sides of the boat, and her knuckles were just a little white. It was a glorious spring day, with a gentle breeze that ruffled the lake. The boat skimmed along faster than ever before, but Janet just felt a *little* tense, not that awful fear she'd felt the first time. She supposed she had Lucas to thank for that.

He jumped out of the boat before they got to the shoreline and pulled it the rest of the way in. When

Janet got out, she tried not to notice that his running shorts were plastered to his body like skin.

"You're doing much better," he said as he tied the boat to a small tree.

"Some." She didn't want to admit that she wasn't scared to death. Then she'd have to explain why she was flushed and shaky.

"Just leave the basket in the boat. I'll take you on a tour of the island, then we can eat."

He took her hand and started along the shore. "This was all part of our place once. I used to hunt rabbits on the bluff."

The island sloped gently to the lake on their side but rose sharply toward the other side. She assumed that was the bluff. It was not a large island, perhaps the size of two football fields, but it was nevertheless an island. She'd never been on an island, and in spite of her resolve to use the time to interrogate Lucas, she wanted to rush around the island, examine every rock and tree, while visions of Long John Silver, castaways and such danced through her head. Oak trees, their tiny new leaves just showing, dotted the land, along with redbuds and dogwood. In places the woods were dense, in other places they thinned out to what might have been meadows at one time. "Any treasure?" When he draped his arm over her shoulders, her arm circled his waist. It seemed a natural part of the magic of the place.

He laughed. "Maybe some beer cans. It's probably a good thing it wasn't an island when I was a kid. I would have built a pirate boat and dug the whole thing up."

"You read Stevenson, too?" She matched his stride, all too aware of his maleness and strength.

"Of course. Followed by all the Hornblower books. I built a raft and loaded up all the barn cats and the dogs as my crew. We set sail on the river one fine morning and sank three feet from shore. The cats never let me near them again. By age twelve I thought I would probably die if I didn't get to run away to sea. Mom in all her wisdom helped me pack my bag."

"Wise lady."

"That wasn't the end of it. She insisted on taking a whole roll of pictures with her trusty Kodak—so she'd have something of me to remember she said—all the while telling me stories of friends of hers who had run away to sea and never been seen again. Or come back minus legs and eyes and hands. Well, I suddenly remembered all sorts of things I needed to do. I told her I thought I ought to stay for the apple harvest. She acted as if she was quite put out that I didn't leave after she'd gone to so much trouble to pack. I'm sure she was about to explode in her effort to keep from laughing."

Janet laughed, delighted in this new carefree man reliving his childhood. "I didn't have any islands. I had a grandmother who collected missionaries. She brought them to our Sunday School class to tell us about the starving children. Looking back I think she did it so we'd eat our spinach. Anyway, this one ancient lady who had spent her life off doing good deeds appeared one Sunday. This enormous voice boomed out of her. 'Food to feed their bellies, bibles to feed their heathen souls, clothes to feed their pagan nakedness,' she told us. Well, I was ready to take my spinach and leave that very day. My mother informed me I had to wait a few years if I wanted to run away and be a missionary. She said she thought cannibals were particularly fond of little girls.''

His laughter rang across the island. "Well, you finally ran away and did it, kind of.''

She laughed. "I guess I did.'' The talk of her missionary effort reminded her of Edgar. "Lucas, why didn't you tell me about Edgar's disability hearing?''

He shrugged. "It's not a sure thing. I just talked to my counterpart in this area and managed to get a hearing. But I see no reason why his claim won't be approved. God knows, he deserves it. It's criminal that he didn't get it the first go round. He'll need a medical checkup, but I think any doctor would agree he'll probably never be able to work again.''

"He couldn't afford a lawyer the first time.''

"Dammit, you shouldn't *need* a lawyer to get disability.'' He kicked a rock ahead of him. "He paid in all his life. It's not like he wanted anyone to give him something. Not that that should make one whit's worth of difference to somebody in need. It's a sorry system.''

She heard a bitterness behind his anger. "Well, I'm glad you did it. I guess that means he won't need us to take care of him anymore. He can afford a retirement home of some sort. He certainly can't live alone again, since that was what exacerbated the stroke to begin with.'' She felt Lucas's body tense as he stopped and turned to her.

"I didn't do it to get rid of him. I did it because it needed to be done." The anger flashing in his eyes gradually changed to something else. "I'd rather talk about you and your burning desire...to become a missionary." His lips touched hers.

Janet felt the now familiar warmth flood through her body. His kiss lingered, and she put a hand on his chest. She could feel his heart beating, matching hers. She knew she had to stop it, now. She was here to question him, not enjoy his kisses. With great effort she opened her mouth to speak. "What about Inez's young man?" she squeaked.

He shook his head and took her hand. They continued along the shore. "I see Mother has been busy."

"She does about as well with secrets as she does with money." More in control now she decided to find out all she could about his activities.

"The kid is a real hard case. The only reason he wants the baby is because his mother wants it. She thinks she'll get some kind of welfare for keeping it."

"Nice. Real nice." Janet never ceased to be appalled at such callousness, although she knew it happened every day.

"See that big white oak over there? I had a tree house there. Every time it rained, the whole thing washed away."

They walked toward the massive tree and Janet could almost see him as a boy, working on his tree house. "What was it made of?"

"A few boards and a lot of cardboard boxes. I was planning to build quite a mansion, but Dad caught me stealing his good lumber, so I was forced to resort to scraps and boxes. It was right up in that crotch." He pointed high into the tree. "It wasn't quite that high when I was a kid. Let's go see the bluff."

She followed him up the steep incline. When they suddenly broke through the treeline, they were high above the lake. The blue-green water spread before them in all its quiet majesty. Crow's Rest perched, tiny and white, off to their right. She felt as if she'd been transported to some magical place, complete with a handsome prince. "It's magnificent. Wouldn't you love to live right here?"

Lucas laughed and squeezed her waist. "Actually, I tried to buy it before the lake filled. The Army Corps of Engineers was at that time willing to sell it. You can't imagine how badly I wanted it. I dreamed about it at night."

"What happened?"

"The only catch was that they wanted a causeway built out to it. It would have cost hundreds of thousands of dollars."

"What a shame." She felt an unreasoning stab of disappointment that he had lost his dream.

"I thought so. I never did figure out their reasoning, and of course they couldn't explain it. Probably somebody in Washington wrote a rule about islands needing causeways and it's been sacred ever since." He was silent for a moment. "Why don't we eat up here? I'll go get the basket."

Janet sat down to wait, gazing out over the water as it moved slowly toward the dam some forty miles away. She thought it would be nice to stay here forever. Beneath her the limestone bluff stretched down to the lake. She wished she could have seen the place before the water rose to hide it. When she heard Lucas coming, she brushed leaves and twigs off a flat limestone rock, which she assumed was a part of the bluff.

He opened the picnic basket. An old lace tablecloth lay on top. "I see Mom wants class maintained in all things." Beneath the tablecloth was a neatly folded, handmade quilt.

Janet spread the quilt, then the tablecloth, and began arranging the containers and packages of food. "Lord, she must have thought we would be out here the rest of the summer."

"Mom likes to prepare for all contingencies. She probably assumed something would happen to the boat and we'd be marooned." He handed her a thick ham sandwich. "It's not a bad idea, is it?"

His voice was light and teasing, but his eyes spoke of other things—the same things she was already trying not to think about. She concentrated on her sandwich, which tasted like cardboard, not through any fault of Bea's. She studied the wealth of food on the checkered tablecloth in order to avoid studying him. "I think those things are the meringue silkies," she said, hoping her voice sounded light and bright.

"That's what I was afraid of. Do you have any idea what they are?"

"Not really. Egg whites and heaven knows what else." Somehow he had moved closer. She fidgeted around on the quilt. She'd been crazy to think she could just come here with him and pass the time of day with tales of their childhoods. She ached for him, craved his nearness. But she had to stay in control. She knew now that she couldn't indulge in a summer romance with him—she loved him too much. And when he left, she would hurt too much.

"Maybe the bass would like them." He sailed one off the bluff and put his sandwich down. "What am I going to do about you, Janet?" His voice was soft and silky.

Janet sailed the rest of her sandwich off the bluff and wondered if she should follow it—which was exactly what was going to happen if she inched any farther off the quilt. "I don't know what you're talking about.

"Don't you?" He stretched out on his side, propped up on one elbow. His fingers stroked her hand.

"Not really." She knew the time had come to put a stop to this. And she fully intended to in a minute if the warmth turned to fire.

"I want you to come back to Little Rock."

"Whatever for?" Lord, was he proposing? Her heart pounded faster.

"Since you're so devoted to Mom, you could look after her just as well there as here."

Disappointment flooded through her. "Oh." She looked out over the lake and felt the tingly warmth wane. He was interested in her as a companion for Bea.

"And I could see you more often." His fingers stroked her arm.

"Oh?" Excitement replaced her disappointment as the warmth flooded back again.

"This certainly is a one-way conversation." He reached up to stroke a wisp of her hair back in place.

"Well . . ." She sat unmoving.

He pulled her down on the quilt. "You are driving me crazy, woman."

"I am?" She felt the warmth turn to a raging fire and race through her body.

"You are. Don't you know how much I want you?"

"No." She knew it couldn't be any more than she wanted him at that moment. Before he could say anything else, she was in his arms, her hands buried in his hair.

"Janet, Janet," he murmured against her ear.

His lips traced a long hot line down her throat and back, and she trembled. When his mouth returned to hers, she yielded to the hot kisses, releasing all her pent-up need and love. If he left tomorrow, she would have today to remember. The fire took her, like a prairie burning in August. Her hands memorized the long sinewy muscles of his back.

"Love me, Janet." His kisses demanded.

She wanted to cry out her love for him. "Lucas, I—"

His fingers touched her lips. "Don't think about tomorrow. There's just today."

She felt the fire recede at his words. She kissed him one last time and pulled away, filled with despair. She'd been so sure he felt more. But in that brief moment of passion she'd known she loved him too much for there not to be a tomorrow. "No, I can't." She felt a tear well up.

"What is it?" He tried to pull her close again.

"I think we'd better go." She began to throw things into the basket.

He held her hands in his. "What is the matter? What did I do? Talk to me, Janet."

"There's nothing to talk about." She refused to look at him.

"That's not good enough, dammit. You want me just as badly as I want you."

"But I want a tomorrow," she said quietly. "I—I can't just—a summer romance won't work for me."

He lifted her face and their eyes met. "Then come back with me. I didn't mean there was no tomorrow, I just meant today was the kind of special time we experience only once."

She didn't think she could explain what she felt to herself, let alone to him. "Oh, Lucas, don't you see? It's just a physical attraction we feel. You want me to uproot Bea and rush off to Little Rock with you. For what? It's more complicated than today."

"To explore what we have, to develop what we feel. I feel something for you that I haven't felt in a long time, maybe never."

She looked at the lake. The sun had begun its long trek to the dark side of the world. The sky shone with a rosy pink softness. It was breathtaking. "And what if we discover there's nothing there?"

"I don't believe that and neither do you."

"What happens to your mother, then?"

He followed her gaze across the lake. "You can't plan your future to the last detail, years ahead, Janet. Life doesn't work that way. You have to take chances."

"I've taken my share of chances, thank you."

"I don't have any intention of hurting you like that jerk of a doctor did. Do you want me to tell you I want to spend the rest of my life with you? I don't know that yet. I don't think you do, either."

"Well, when you find out, look me up."

"Dammit, I can't know that until I know you better. Don't let an old hurt kill a beautiful possibility, Janet. And don't hide behind Mother."

"We need to go." She finished the packing and stood up.

"You are a stubborn woman."

"Right," she replied and started walking, ignoring all the things that an hour ago had seemed so magical. She got in the boat and faced away from him, unwilling to look at him, unwilling to take the chance that she would weaken and agree to go with him. Unwilling to admit that he had offered her a chance for love and happiness and she had demanded forever. Hadn't she been the one who had told him nothing is forever? She had tried her best to force him into a commitment *she* wasn't even ready to make.

She tried, more times than once on the endless ride home, to turn and tell him she'd been wrong tell him she wanted to try. And perhaps if it hadn't involved uprooting Bea, she could have, would have. But if she took the leap, it also meant Bea had to take the leap. And despite what he said, it was a real concern. She wasn't hiding behind anything. If he wanted a relationship, they could do it long-distance. Other people did. No, he wanted her in Little Rock because he wanted Bea in Little Rock.

When they reached the dock, she jumped out of the boat and almost ended up in the lake. She snatched at the basket, but Lucas was ahead of her. He took the basket in one hand, her arm in the other.

"This is not over, Janet. You think about it, and when you can quit wallowing in that old hurt, let me know."

His eyes held a mixture of anger, hurt, desire. She pulled away and headed for the house. When she looked up, Bea was waving frantically from the porch. Janet sighed, wondering what new disaster awaited her to cap off an already lousy day.

"Oh, Janet, I thought you'd never get back."

Janet was suddenly alert. "What is it?"

Bea's voice sounded fluttery. "Inez is in labor."

"Oh, Lord. Have you called the ambulance?"

"There was a terrible wreck out west of town. They're all out there. They'll come as soon as they can."

Janet started past Bea. "Well, I'm sure we have plenty of time."

Lucas caught her arm. "What can I do?"

She saw the concern in his eyes, and her ache for him welled up again. "Oh, I don't know. Go boil some water."

CHAPTER NINE

JANET MADE IT to Inez's room behind the kitchen in record time, with Bea puffing at her back. As she entered the room, she took a long, deep breath and called up all she remembered about obstetrics, hoping against hope that she wouldn't be called on to use it. She would get Inez bundled up, and they would drive her to the hospital, not wait for the ambulance. She smiled as she took the girl's hand. "How long have the contractions been coming, Inez?"

The girl's eyes were wide with fear. "Long time. I didn't want to bother Bea."

She stroked the girl's sweat-drenched forehead. "How far apart are they? Do you know?" At that moment Inez was seized with a contraction. Her face contorted, and she clung to Janet's hand. "Deep breaths, sweetie, deep breaths." She checked her watch as the contraction passed. "Good. Now I'm going to check you and see how far along you are. Okay? Then we're going to drive you to the hospital."

She pulled the sheet back and gently maneuvered the girl into the examination position. Inez was fully dilated, she saw with a sinking feeling.

Bea held Inez's hand. "What are we going to do?"

Janet gave them both a smile that she hoped conveyed a confidence she didn't really feel. "It looks like we're going to deliver this baby." A glance at Bea told her the woman was too flushed. Her heart was probably having a field day. Inez tensed with another contraction. Two minutes apart. "Bea, go get clean sheets and towels please, and boil some water."

"Oh, but I can't leave her." Bea mopped at the girl's face with a wet washcloth.

"Send Lucas in here. You take care of the other things." Bea bustled out. Janet doubted Lucas would be any help at all, but she couldn't run the risk of Bea getting overly excited and having an attack.

"What should I do?" He was beside her, looking a little uncomfortable and slightly green around the gills.

"Breathe with her. Deep breaths. And hold her hand when the pain hits. She's scared to death." She wanted to add she was, too, but didn't think it would inspire confidence. She stopped to wipe her own sweat-drenched hands and face. She had watched plenty of deliveries during her training, but watching in a fully-equipped room full of specialists and doing it herself were two very different things.

"Mom's boiling water. I didn't know you really did that."

"You don't. It's what they used to do to give fathers something to do besides pass out. Now breathe with her." She watched him take deep breaths, a little self-consciously at first, then settle into a rhythm. When the next contraction hit, he held Inez's hand and breathed and encouraged her.

"It hurts so bad, Janet. I can't stand it," Inez moaned.

Janet felt the girl's pain and wished she could help her. At least Inez wouldn't have the trauma of long hours in labor. "I know, honey. But there's just not a lot of choice when things get started. It won't be long. When I say push, bear down, okay?" She looked at Lucas. "She's coming. Or maybe he. Oh, what the heck, if *she's* sure it's a girl, so am I. Push, Inez, push hard. Come on, bear down. Okay, rest a minute." The baby's head lay in her sweaty hand. Janet smiled at the tiny, wrinkled face and struggled to control her rush of emotions. "I have her. One more big push." She gently rotated the baby until a shoulder appeared, then the other. "Come on, come on, almost there." A second later, she held the baby girl in her hands. "Ah, we were right. You have your little girl, Inez."

Janet cleared the baby's nostrils and held her up. A lusty squall broke the silence. As she looked up, her eyes met those of Lucas. She saw in his eyes something of the awe she knew must be in her own. They had shared a moment . . . a miracle.

Bea bustled in at that moment, carrying an armful of towels and a pair of scissors dangling from the kitchen tongs. "I remembered the scissors, Janet. And the clamps old Doctor Sterling gave me, just in case." She stopped. "Oh, it's over. I missed it."

Janet grinned. "Bless old Doctor Sterling, whoever he is. I'm glad you remembered." After finishing up, she lay the baby on Inez's stomach. Her hands trembled. "She's perfect, Inez. All her toes, all her fingers, and she doesn't look one bit like Clarence." The girl smiled, and Janet saw something different in her eyes, a calm and intelligence she hadn't seen before. The fear was gone.

"Thank you, Janet. Oh, thank you for my baby."

"Hey, you did all the work." She was suddenly conscious of Lucas standing perfectly still, staring at her. She gently placed a clean towel over the baby. "We'll let you two have a few more minutes together, then we'll clean everybody up a little." She scrutinized Bea. "Are you all right, Bea?"

Bea collapsed in a chair beside the bed. "I'm just fine, dear. Just fine. It's been a wonderful evening."

She decided the older woman was, in fact, just fine, then carried towels and things to the kitchen, anxious to be alone to try and pull herself together, knowing Bea would hover over Inez and the baby like a mother hen. Now that it was over, it was time to fall to pieces. Have a nice quiet nervous breakdown. She stood at the sink, gulping air in great breaths.

"That was pretty impressive," Lucas said quietly behind her. "You're a real pro."

She turned toward him and tried to smile. "That's my first one. And I hope my last."

"You did fine."

A tear coursed down Janet's cheek. "Inez did fine. But what if something had gone wrong? I'm not a midwife." She trembled with shock.

"But it didn't." Suddenly his arms were around her, holding her tight. "Hey, it's all over now. You were great."

She clung to him and sobbed against his chest, whether from her awe at the miracle she'd helped bring into the world or from her relief that nothing awful had happened, she wasn't sure. He held her and stroked her hair and told her that things were going to be fine. Which made her sob all the more in the warm safety of his arms. As he stroked her back, she finally began to calm. When the doorbell rang, she pulled away and wiped her face. "The paramedics, no doubt."

"Shall I send them on their way?"

"No. I want Inez and the baby to go in to the hospital. The baby's eyes need treatment, there are blood tests, and a pediatrician needs to check her over. And I want Inez checked, too." Arm in arm they went to the door.

Two young men in starched white uniforms, lugging an array of satchels and paraphernalia stood at the door. Lucas grinned at them. "You're a little late. We did it ourselves."

One of the young men returned his grin. "Usually fathers fall apart. You okay?"

Janet laughed at Lucas's look of confusion. "Daddy here is doing just fine."

Lucas seemed, for the first time, at a loss for words. "I'm not . . . I'm fine."

"We got here as soon as we could, but there was a really bad pileup on the new bypass. Bad news."

Janet stepped in. "I think mother and baby are fine, but I want them checked. I'll follow you to the hospital." She led the way to Inez's room.

"Do I have to go to the hospital, Janet?" Inez objected when they all appeared in the doorway. She looked as if she would be content to lie there with her baby forever.

Janet almost weakened at the sight, then smiled and nodded. "Yes, I'm afraid you do."

After they loaded Inez and her baby in the ambulance, Lucas led Janet to the door. "I'll take you. I don't think you're in any condition to drive."

"I'm fine."

"You're still shaking."

"I'm not shaking," she said, trying to find the sleeve of her windbreaker, which somehow kept flittering away. She felt embarrassed over her crying jag in the kitchen. "I'll probably be there all night."

"So I'll come back and get you in the morning." He helped her into the jacket and steered her toward the car.

"It's not really necessary." But she was glad he was going. She had a feeling she wouldn't even be able to figure out how to start the car let alone drive it to town. She took a few deep breaths and tried to stop shaking.

"I don't mind. After all, this baby is part mine."

"I guess it is at that. By the way, thanks for your help."

"Well, it was an interesting experience, but not one I'd care to repeat anytime soon." He pulled out of the driveway. "I don't suppose she has any medical insurance."

"You suppose right, but a checkup will be a lot cheaper than a delivery and certainly a lot cheaper than a delivery with complications. We were lucky. And we'll manage."

He lapsed into quietness. Janet lay her head against the seat and felt some of the shakiness and tension begin to slip away.

"What would have happened if you hadn't been there?"

She roused herself at the question. "The baby would have come, anyway. It would have been a lot harder on Inez, but I think she would have managed. Why?"

"It's scary, that's all." He lapsed back into silence.

Janet lay back for a moment, then looked over at him with dawning realization of what he was talking about. "You're thinking it could have been Bea, right?"

"Janet, it took the ambulance well over an hour to get there."

"I think that's just . . . a freak thing. There was a wreck."

"There are a lot of wrecks."

Janet sighed. The magic of the birth suddenly seemed overshadowed by the specter of a crisis that would end, not with the miracle of new life but with the end of an elderly woman's life. She shifted uncomfortably in the seat. "I know."

"I'm sorry to ruin the evening, but I can't help thinking about it."

"I know." Fortunately at that moment, they pulled up at the emergency room entrance. She started to jump out of the car before he could say anything else. "I'll call you when we're ready." He caught her arm and pulled her across the seat. His kiss was gentle and as sweet as morning dew. In that instant she tumbled down the pathway of love into a realm she had only dreamed about.

"Thank you for being there, love," he murmured.

Then he was gone. Janet watched the taillights disappear, unwilling to move and break the spell of his kiss.

She passed a restless night in the hospital, seeing to Inez, assuring her she would get her baby back, mostly worrying. Worrying about that sweet kiss, worrying that her love and need for Lucas were palpable things now. Worrying about what he'd said. Because she knew it was true. It could have been Bea. And delivering a baby was quite a different matter from treating a heart attack. She finally dozed in a fitful sleep on the cot in Inez's room.

When a hand touched her cheek, she came awake at once. And saw Lucas bending over her. "Did I call?"

He smiled. "No, but Mom couldn't wait."

Janet looked across the room. Bea was busying around Inez, talking a mile a minute. "What time is it?"

"A little before eight. It looks like you had a bad night."

She sighed and got up, trying to stretch the kinks out of her back. "I have had better nights, I must admit." He rubbed her back with a strong yet gentle hand. "Oh, that feels good." She leaned into his hand. There was a new intimacy to his touch. They had shared a miracle, and it had in some subtle way changed them both.

"How about some coffee?"

"Umm. Preferably right into a vein." She ran her fingers through her hair, knowing she looked like death warmed over, but somehow she didn't have the energy to care.

"Mom, we're going to the cafeteria."

"Run along, dear. I'll take care of the new mother. We're trying to decide on a name. Oh, dear, isn't it exciting?"

Lucas took Janet's arm and led her into the hall. "That should keep them busy for the rest of the day."

When they were seated in the hospital cafeteria with hot coffee, Janet began to come to life, although her eyes felt as if someone had sandpapered them. "What are you doing here so early? We probably won't be able to get Inez discharged before ten."

"As soon as the stores open we're going to go buy them out, I think. At least that's the impression I got from the list Mom's been working on since daylight." He sipped coffee. "Are you all right?" He touched her cheek with his finger.

"Nothing a little sleep in a real bed won't fix." She squinted her eyes. "Listen, about our talk last night?" She felt a need to clear the air between them so that she could enjoy her new feelings.

"Forget it."

She blinked at him and wished her eyes weren't so scratchy. "You bring it up, I worry about it all night, and you say forget it?"

"I was overwhelmed by all the excitement."

She looked at him, a frown on her face. He wasn't the type to be overwhelmed by anything. "Well, all I was going to say was, it worries me, too, but I still think it has to be Bea's decision. If the isolation doesn't worry her, I don't think it should worry us."

He shrugged. "Maybe. If you're that worried about it, you can both come back to Little Rock with me."

"You're not listening."

His hand covered hers. "I'm listening, but I don't think you are."

Maybe it was the lack of sleep, but she couldn't figure out what he was talking about. "You haven't said anything." The pressure on her hand increased.

"I'm asking you to come back with me."

"And I'm saying Bea has to make that decision." Why was he so darned stubborn? "You could move here if you're so worried." She closed her eyes and waited for some response.

"I have a career, such as it is."

She nodded. The message was loud and clear. He wanted it on his terms. Meaning, perhaps, that it would be easier to get rid of her in Little Rock than in his old home place. If she wanted him, she had to settle for a summer romance or go to Little Rock, and she couldn't do that. "Well, so do I."

"Janet, I—" He stood up. "I guess I'd better get Mom off to her shopping spree."

They walked to Inez's room. Janet's step was heavier on the way back than it had been earlier. An aide had brought the baby to nurse, and Inez positively glowed with happiness. Janet did her best to share in the happiness, but her mind was on Lucas and how she was going to get herself out of love.

It seemed like hours until they finally got home, more hours till they got the car unloaded and Inez and the baby to bed. At long last Janet went to her room and collapsed, too tired to get out of her clothes. Too tired to think about Lucas and the mess she had managed to get herself into.

It was late afternoon before she awoke. She was still tired, but she felt better. As she showered, she decided she mostly felt hungry. She went down the stairs with visions of bacon and eggs and biscuits dancing through her head. Bea was making tea and cookies in the kitchen. "I'm starved," she announced.

"Oh, there you are, my dear. I was going to wake you for tea. How do you feel?"

"Much better. How are Inez and the baby?"

"Just beautiful. Oh, Janet, you were wonderful."

"It wasn't much." She looked out the kitchen window, wondering where Lucas was.

"Oh, but it was. Inez and I are still fussing over a name. She's holding out for Beatrice, and I'm holding out for Janet. I do think Beatrice is such an old-fashioned name, don't you?"

"It's a lovely name. I'll cast my vote for it." Janet was secretly pleased but a little embarrassed that Bea wanted Inez to name the baby after her.

"But I think she should name the baby after you."

"Janet is such a common name, Bea. She should stick with Beatrice." She munched a leftover muffin, noting that she was getting tired of leftover muffins. They would have to come up with something a little more interesting for breakfast. Clarence glared at her from his perch near the muffins. But she was too tired to even scold him.

"Well, I just can't imagine what we would have done if you hadn't been here, dear."

Janet searched the refrigerator for orange juice, wondering if she should broach the subject she'd worried over so much. "Bea, what if it had been you?"

"Me? Well, my dear, it wasn't, was it?" She put water on to boil.

"But if it had been?"

"You're beginning to sound like Lucas, dear."

Janet sipped orange juice and studied the older woman. Finally she gently led Bea to a chair and kneeled in front of her. "Bea, it could have been you, with an attack and no ambulance." Bea smiled and reached out a hand to touch Janet's face. Her clear blue eyes softened.

"Janet, dear, I thought you understood, but I see you don't. Of course, I don't expect Lucas to understand, but—"

"Bea, we're talking about—"

"I know what we're talking about, dear. We're talking about an old woman dropping dead before you can get her to the hospital. You're too young to realize that there are so many things worse than that. I've had a wonderful life, my dear, absolutely wonderful, and when my time comes, I'll be ready."

"But—"

"Oh, you dear, sweet child, you've been worrying yourself silly over nothing." She looked out the kitchen window, a dreamy smile on her face and in her eyes. "You can't possibly understand what these past few weeks have meant to me. To feel needed again. To have something to get up for in the morning. To have life and laughter in this old house again. If I go tomorrow, it will have been worth it. The greatest wish my dear Jake had was to die in harness. And he did, pruning the roses. It's the way I would choose, too." She focused on Janet. "Don't worry about me, dear. I'm good for many more years."

Janet nodded, unable to speak at the moment. She bussed the older woman on the cheek and went back to her juice and muffin, deeply moved by Bea's unwavering belief in how things were meant to be. "Well, where is everybody?"

Bea resumed her bustling. "Edgar is somewhere outside. You can't imagine how excited he is about the baby. Verla is creating a blizzard of snowflakes. She's moved on to chartreuse—quite frightening, really. Not Verla, of course, but the fact that anyone in their right senses would make chartreuse snowflakes. I believe she has in mind to attach them and make a snowflake blanket for the baby. Mrs. Heunfield checked out, and Mr. Bradley is painting our picture. The new guest who called to say she would be a day late called to say she would be another day. It appears she's lost somewhere in western Oklahoma. I tried to give her directions, but it just seemed to confuse her all the more." She removed a tray of chocolate chip cookies from the oven.

"And Lucas?"

"Well, that's most peculiar. He rushed off this morning to the airport. Something about having to check something out in Little Rock. He should be back this afternoon. Oh, it is afternoon, isn't it? Well, I'm sure he'll be back soon.''

Janet wondered what he'd gone to Little Rock for on such short notice. Probably to reserve a room in some dreary retirement home. Well, everything was much clearer to Janet after her conversation with Bea. She would stay because that's what Bea wanted. If it meant giving up Lucas, so be it, although she couldn't really give up what she'd never had. But after talking to Bea, her doubts had vanished, and she knew they were doing the right thing. His invitation to Little Rock was strictly so that he would have a companion for Bea—which was a moot point now that Bea wasn't going anywhere—and perhaps a brief affair with Janet. At least she assumed it was. After the picnic there had been no more teasing kisses, no more talk of... anything. He had been nice, charming, distant. True, there'd been little time for anything else, what with Inez. But she would never forget that soul-searing kiss in the hospital parking lot...different from all the other ones...

''Dear, tea is ready. Would you call Edgar and Verla? I'll take a nice tray to Inez.''

''Sure.'' Janet managed to untangle Verla from her chartreuse snowflakes then went out to call Edgar. He was not on the porch. She checked the garden and the outbuildings, but he was nowhere to be found. She felt the first nibbles of panic as she raced upstairs to check his room. Nothing. She raced back to the kitchen. ''Bea, when did you see Edgar last?''

''Earlier in the afternoon. I'm not sure.''

"I can't find him." She tried to keep her panic at bay, telling herself he had just gone for a walk. He hadn't had a spell since he'd started helping with the garden.

"Oh dear. Did you check the dock? He does like to sit out there."

Janet raced toward the dock, Bea trundling along after her. She checked the boat house, but he wasn't there. She was on her way toward the house when she stopped dead in her tracks and hurried back to the boat house. Edgar wasn't there and neither was the aluminum boat.

CHAPTER TEN

"WHERE WOULD HE have gone, Bea?" Janet tried to calm the woman, who now stood on the dock in tears.

"I don't know. Fishing?"

"Do you have any idea where?"

"Maybe to the island. He used to live over that way."

"Bea, don't worry. We'll find him. He's probably gone to visit someone across the lake." She said the words but she didn't believe them for a minute. "After all, he's been around boats and water all his life. Is there anyone we can call? Somebody who patrols the lake?"

Bea shook her head. "It's all my fault, I should have kept a closer eye on him. But he's been doing so well, I just thought . . . oh dear."

"It's not your fault, Bea." She glanced at the boat house, at the little wooden boat. The boat that she was going to have to get in and go search for Edgar. She felt the old tension rise and grow, threatening to overwhelm her. Where the heck was Lucas when they needed him? "I'm going to go look for him, Bea."

Bea wiped her tears and stood up straight. "I'll go with you."

"No you won't. I'll probably drown myself, and there's no reason for you to drown, too. Besides, somebody needs to stay here in case Lucas gets back. So that he can come rescue the rescuer."

"Oh, but I know how you feel about water."

"I'll do just fine. Don't worry." She thought that at that moment she was doing quite enough worrying for both of them. She pulled the boat close to the dock and stepped into it. It rocked wildly, and she almost lost her balance *and* her muffins. "Do you have any idea how you start this thing, Bea?" she asked, knowing full well that Bea would know little more about it than she did.

"No, dear. There must be a switch somewhere."

Janet examined the trolling motor thoroughly and discovered several switches and knobs, none of which had labels or instructions. She began twisting them and fiddling, thinking that eventually she would hit the right combination, cursing herself for facing the front during her training sessions.

"Janet, there's the boat!" Bea screamed.

Janet turned to follow Bea's pointing finger. She shaded her eyes and saw the aluminum boat, rocking gently near the island. It appeared to be empty. "Oh no, please don't let it be," she muttered, yanking switches with new abandon. She was rewarded with a hum, and the boat slammed into the dock, almost knocking her into the water. She grabbed the handle she'd seen Lucas use and wiggled it, turning the boat. "Call somebody, Bea. Anybody," she yelled as she left the dock and zigzagged toward the distant island. "Maybe the Coast Guard has a unit around here." She doubted that seriously, but it would give Bea something to worry about besides Edgar.

She fiddled with more adjustments until she got more speed, and hung on to the motor and the boat. And her stomach. She tried not to think about being in a boat by herself, she tried only to think about Edgar and what on earth she was going to do when she got to his boat. There was no way she could dive into the lake and search for him. No way. "Please let him be taking a nap," she muttered.

When she finally got close, she realized she didn't know how to turn the motor off, so she just raised it out of the water and let it run. She drifted close enough to the aluminum boat to peek in then bumped it with her boat. Edgar was curled up on the bottom of the boat sleeping. She sighed with relief and maneuvered her boat alongside the other until she could reach over and touch him. "Edgar, wake up."

Nothing happened for a long moment, then the old man came up flailing his arms like a windmill. "What? What?" Both boats rocked violently.

It took her so by surprise, all she could do was to hang on. Then she saw the angry red lump on his head. He must have fallen and hurt himself. "Edgar, it's me. It's Janet. You're in a boat, Edgar." Oh, Lord, he was going to dump them both, and she was going to drown. Edgar probably knew how to swim. He shook his head and looked at her with clear blue eyes. She sighed with relief.

"Oh. Miz Janet. What are you doin' out here?" He stepped toward her and the aluminum boat tipped. He fell across the edge, half in and half out.

Janet grabbed for him, missed, grabbed again. "Not so fast, Edgar." She got hold of his arm and pulled, almost upsetting the wooden boat in the process.

"Whew. I'm a little dizzy."

"You bumped your head. Can you make it to this boat?" She pulled again. He began to clamber from one boat to the other, missed his hold and fell into the water.

"I guess I didn't make it, did I?" he asked when his head appeared again.

She smiled and tried to tell herself she was going to get them both back home safely—as soon as she figured out how. "No problem, Edgar."

"What're you doin' out on the lake? You wasn't looking for me, was you?"

"It's a long story, Edgar. Do you think you can climb in?" The boat rocked sickeningly.

"I don't know. I'm afraid she'll tip over."

Janet agreed wholeheartedly with that assumption, but didn't want to frighten the man, although he seemed a lot calmer than she was at this point. "What are we going to do?"

He looked toward the island, calm as could be. "Just put the motor in and go toward the island. I'll hang on till we get to shallow water."

"Good idea." At least it seemed like a good idea. They were close to the island, close enough to swim— if she knew how to swim. She lowered the motor into the water and finally got the boat aimed for the island. About twenty feet out, Edgar was virtually jogging alongside the boat.

"Cut her off, Miz Janet. Cut her off," he yelled as she passed him.

"I don't know how," she yelled back as the boat careered toward the island, missing the sandy part where she and Lucas had landed. She closed her eyes and held on as the boat rammed a rocky ledge. Something in the motor screeched as she fell over the side. She came up spluttering and flailing, then discovered she was in about three feet of water.

"That was a right smart landing, Miz Janet, but I think you sheared a pin in the motor." Edgar helped her up, and they waded to the ledge.

"What does that mean?" She didn't care what it meant as long as she was on dry land again.

The old man smiled. "I reckon it means we might just as well enjoy the sunset, 'cause we're not goin' anywhere."

"Oh." She spit out lake water and tried to wring as much as she could out of her hair and clothes. "That's what I thought it meant." They perched on the rock, side by side. Janet was glad the day had been warm. The rock radiated heat. She didn't want to think about what they would do if nobody came before night.

"I reckon I got us into some kind of mess, didn't I?"

She squeezed the man's hand. "Think of it more as an adventure, Edgar. Do you remember taking the boat out?"

He nodded. "I been feelin' so good, I thought I'd just go for a little spin. I was doin' just fine till I dropped my hat. Somehow my feet got all tangled up when I bent over to pick it up."

"You must have fallen and hit your head." She leaned over and gently touched the lump. He had taken quite a fall, judging from its size.

"I guess I came to, but I was kinda dizzy, so I just thought I'd rest awhile, then go back. Guess I went to sleep."

"And I scared you half to death, crashing into you. Let me look at your head." She carefully examined the lump, then looked into his eyes. No sign of fixed pupils. She held up one finger. "How many fingers, Edgar?"

"One."

"Good." She moved her finger back and forth and watched his eyes track it. "Who's the president?"

"Woodrow Wilson."

Janet swallowed hard. "Edgar—"

The old man grinned. "Just teasin', Miz Janet. And my name's Edgar Guinn, and my momma's name was Priscilla, and we're settin' on what used to be the nicest apple orchard in this part of the country."

Janet hugged Edgar tight, relieved that the bump on the head was nothing serious. "Great, Edgar. No sign of concussion. And you know what? I think you're going to be just fine. Just fine, Edgar." She kissed his cheek. "Now, tell me about the time you took Harry S. Truman to every whistle-stop between here and New Orleans."

"Oh, my, I wish you coulda seen that train, Miz Janet. Pretty as a picture, she was."

Janet lay back on the rock and listened to the story she had heard many times, but somehow it was different today. More real. Edgar was telling it, not living it. He described every stop, what Mr. Truman had worn, what Bess had worn, how the people had clapped and whistled and cheered. She could almost see it.

"Anyhow, when we got to Mena—"

Janet sensed the change in Edgar and sat up quickly. "What is it?"

"It's Luke in that little sailboat. I'll swear, look at that thing fly."

She shaded her eyes against the setting sun and saw the sail. It was a beautiful sight against the pink sky. The sailboat seemed to fly over the water, the sail billowing in the evening breeze. The hero, coming to rescue us, she thought. Then she thought how annoyed he would probably be with her for wrecking his motor. Then she thought about how annoyed *she* was going to be when she told him how they'd come to be so wet and he started laughing. After all, if he'd been where he was supposed to be instead of off looking at retirement homes, *he* could have rescued Edgar. She stood up and waved, so that he would know they were okay. Edgar waved, too, and whooped and laughed with delight at the swift sailboat skimming toward them.

Janet saw Lucas do something to the sail and it seemed to collapse as he neared the island. Then the boat nudged into the deeper water on the far side of the ledge and Lucas was out of the boat. She was in his arms before she knew what had happened.

"Are you all right?" He smothered her with kisses.

His concern touched her so deeply, she almost cried. "We're fine, but I'm glad you're here. I think I hurt your boat."

"I don't care about the boat." He brushed kisses against her ear and whispered, "Too bad Edgar's here. We could stay marooned together. All night." He held on to her when she struggled to get free. "You okay, Edgar?"

"Fine as can be, Luke, thanks to Miz Janet."

Janet broke away from Lucas, embarrassed by the display they'd made in front of Edgar, afraid her wet clothes were steaming from his kisses. "There's no need to get so worked up. I had everything under control all along," she quipped, trying to lighten things up.

He pulled her close and kissed her again, sweetly and gently, then burst into laughter. "So I see. I guess you just decided since it was such a nice day, you'd take a swim in your clothes, right?" He ducked her swat. "Edgar, let's get these boats tied up. I'll come tow them tomorrow."

She watched them secure the two flat-bottom boats, a sinking feeling in the pit of her stomach. "Are we all going back in that?" She pointed toward the little sailboat.

"She'll carry us just fine. Surely you don't have any qualms after what you've been through."

"It leans."

"I'll keep her as steady as a rocking chair." His eyes danced with mischief.

With great misgivings she got into the sailboat. "I could stay on the island tonight, ride back with you in the morning." Lucas seated her beside the wheel. Edgar crouched in the prow.

Lucas's lips brushed her ear. "Didn't I tell you about the bears that live on the island?"

"No you didn't, but I think I'd rather take my chances with the bears." He put the sail up and maneuvered out into the lake. Janet clung to a railing, waiting for the boat to lean. When it didn't, she relaxed a little. As the boat skimmed the water, she relaxed enough to enjoy the new sensation. Halfway across the lake, she fell in love with sailing. She felt as if they were flying through the air, the only sound being the flapping sail and the breeze. She felt free and disconnected from the earth. She closed her eyes and let the breeze wash over her.

Lucas touched her cheek. "Nice, isn't it?"

"I can't believe it. I've never experienced anything like it in my life." Her cares and the tension of the afternoon flew away on the fresh evening breeze.

"It was only after I got a sailboat that I truly understood why men have always gone down to the sea in ships. I would give my eyeteeth to round the Cape on a Clipper ship."

She smiled up at him. "I think they *really* lean too much. I got sick watching *Moby Dick*."

"That probably had more to do with the lurching of the whale than the leaning of the ship." He stroked her neck and whispered, his breath mingling with the fresh breeze. "You should try sleeping on a boat. It's a sleep unlike any other. The quietness of the night, the gentle rocking of the boat." His lips brushed her neck. "I want to make love to you tonight, Janet. Out on the lake, under the stars.''

"Lucas! Edgar's right over there.''

"Edgar would approve the idea wholeheartedly.''

"Isn't this boat a little small?'' Right now, she fully expected Lucas to drop Edgar off and head back out in the lake. And right now she would go with him and love him under the stars. She would worry about tomorrow some other time.

"I'll get a bigger boat.'' The fantasy ended when he had to bring in the sail. Janet felt a stab of disappointment.

A breathless Bea waited on the dock. She led them to the house, fussing about hot soup and dry clothes. Janet ran up to change while Lucas saw to Edgar. When she got back to the kitchen, Bea was sitting in the rocking chair, breathing heavily.

"Bea, what is it?''

"Nothing, dear, just a little angina. Could you get my pills?''

Janet noted the flush as she got a nitroglycerin tablet and slipped it under Bea's tongue. "Let me check your pressure.'' She quickly checked the blood pressure. It was high. Respiration shallow, pulse thready. "Bea, is there any pain in your arm, any pain in your chest different from the angina?''

"It's nothing. Just a little too much excitement for an old woman.'' She clung to Janet's hand. "You won't tell Lucas, will you?''

"Bea, I don't think there's a thing to worry about, but we're going to the hospital to get an EKG. You've had a lot of excitement and worry today and we need a record of whatever is going on right now." She smiled with a brightness she didn't feel. "So we can plan your excitement more carefully in the future. If we'd known how upset you were, Edgar and I would have just swum home." She hoped the chatter would relax Bea.

"No, please. It will pass."

"Let's just be on the safe side, huh?" She hurried to the stairs and called Lucas. She tried to control the panic in her voice, but she saw it mirrored in his face as he bounded down the stairs.

"What happened?"

She put a hand on his arm. "It's probably just an angina attack, but I think we should take Bea to the emergency room. Just to be sure it's nothing more."

"Oh, God, she's having a heart attack, isn't she? Let's go."

"Call an ambulance."

"No, I won't wait for an ambulance. I'll take her myself."

Janet started to argue that the paramedics were better equipped to deal with the situation if Bea worsened but thought better of it and nodded when she saw the pain on his face. "It's not life threatening. I'm sure of that." She squeezed his hand. "Lucas, she's going to be just fine." Janet hoped with all her heart that her diagnosis was correct. They put Bea in the car and for the second time in as many days headed for the emergency room.

Janet watched as the emergency room staff hooked up the EKG and telemetry pack to monitor Bea's heart. Lucas paced the hall. She motioned for him when the doctor ordered Bea up to the cardiac care unit. Janet stopped the gurney long enough to hug Bea before they took her to the elevator. "It's going to be just fine, Bea."

The older woman smiled dreamily through the painkiller. "Why Janet, dear, I've known that all along. It's not my time yet." Janet joined Lucas and the doctor.

"I'd like to send her to the Springdale hospital for some diagnostic work. They have the capability we don't. It seems she's had a very mild attack," the young doctor told them. "But it's hard to say how much damage may have occurred because of scarring from the last one. We need a series of more sophisticated tests than we can run here. But she's in no immediate danger, I assure you."

Janet listened to Lucas's endless questions, very few of which the doctor could answer until he did further tests. "I'm going up to see Bea," she finally said after half an hour.

Bea was looking much more alert, which indicated that it had, indeed, been a very mild attack, if it was really a heart attack at all. "Feeling better now?"

"Oh, this is such a tiresome thing, but I'm feeling much better. My, what did they give me? It felt very strange. When can I go home?"

"The doctor wants to send you to Springdale for some tests."

"Phooey. I don't need tests."

"Bea, there are new treatments, new procedures. You ought to do it."

"Well, maybe..."

They talked about everything except the attack and by the time Lucas arrived in the company of Bea's family doctor, Bea had dozed off. "She's asleep."

The doctor smiled his best bedside smile. "Good. You two might as well go home. We'll take good care of her. The air ambulance will be here at eight in the morning."

"Air ambulance?" Janet asked, although she didn't need to. She knew what Lucas had decided.

"I'm taking her to Little Rock for the tests," he said quietly, scanning her face for some reaction.

Janet nodded. "Well, that's a good place to go for this sort of thing." She started out of the room.

Lucas caught up to her, looked into her eyes for a long moment, then wrapped his arms around her, holding her tightly to him. "I have to do this."

They stood melded together for an interminable minute, each touching the other's pain. "I know." She clung to him, not wanting to ask the next question, unable to stop herself. "Will you bring her back?"

He cradled her head to his chest, stroking her hair. "I don't know."

Janet felt his heart beat against her own and wanted to cry out her love, but it was neither the time nor the place. Her stomach knotted up when he kissed her fiercely then released her and started out of the hospital. He might not know the answer, but she did. "Bea and I talked about this a few days ago. When she's better, I think you should talk to her."

"Talk about what?" He handed her into the car.

"About how she feels about life."

"I know how she feels, Janet, but what am I supposed to do? Just sit back and wait for the big one to hit her and hope to hell you're there, or the paramedics aren't off at some wreck? Wait for the phone call? I can't do that. When all the tests are done, we'll see."

Janet was grateful for the darkness of the car. She heard the pain in his voice, knew it was in his eyes. She thought he could have handled Bea's attack if it hadn't been for the baby and the ambulance delay. Two traumas in as many days had been just too much. "Well, let me know what you want me to do about the place." She heard the strain in her voice.

"Can you handle things alone?"

"Sure. Inez will be up in another day or two, and she's anxious to help." They were silent until he pulled into the driveway and got out. Janet hurried toward the house, but Lucas caught her arm.

"Janet, I don't know what to say." He pulled her close. "I have to take her to Little Rock. I have to do it."

She held him tightly, knowing it might be for the last time. "I know."

"Will you come to Little Rock when things settle down?"

"I don't know." She swallowed the tears that tried to well up. They should have been out on the lake, exploring their love instead of being here like this, wracked with pain, saying a goodbye that might be final. She'd sensed in recent days that he would not press Bea to move, but all that had changed now. There was little question in her mind that Bea would stay in Little Rock.

"I want you to come. Oh, dammit, there is so much I want to say to you."

"Lucas, this is not the time to think about anything but what's best for Bea." She reached up and touched his cheek. "Bring her back, Lucas. Please bring her back." She felt him stiffen.

"Good night, Janet. And thank you for everything."

She ran up the stairs. He'd made it sound so final. The days and weeks would pass and one day she would get the call, telling her to begin closing things down, that Bea had decided to stay. It would be so impersonal, so...awful. He would settle back into his job and life, and whatever he'd felt for her would be a lost memory. And she would hurt. Oh, how she would hurt. She wrapped herself tightly in the memory of his embrace.

CHAPTER ELEVEN

JANET STAYED in her room the next morning until Lucas left. She couldn't face him, because she knew she would have to plead her case again to bring Bea home. It might end with things being said that couldn't be taken back. When she heard the car leave, she went down to the kitchen to prepare breakfast. To her surprise, Inez had coffee cake in the oven and the table set. "Inez, what are you doing out of bed?"

The girl smiled. "I'm fine this morning. A little sore, but just fine. And it's high time I started pulling my weight around here."

Janet couldn't believe the change in Inez. "Well, don't overdo. You need to take it easy for a few days."

"How is Bea?"

"She's on her way to Little Rock for tests."

Inez sat down with a cup of coffee. "Will she come back?"

Janet smiled. "I don't know. It depends on the tests. And on Lucas."

"I don't know what I would have done without her, and you. I want to thank you for putting up with me. I guess I was a real pain, wasn't I?"

Janet laughed. "You did tend toward trying at times."

"I was so scared. I guess I just wanted to go back to being a little girl and have someone take care of me. That way I could pretend none of it was happening. But it's all okay now."

"I know. How's the little one—or is it little Beatrice—this morning?"

"It's little Beatrice, and she's full as a tick and sleeping. Edgar's in there watching her. He held her this morning. He's as gentle as a lamb. She'll know more about trains by the time she's a week old than most people ever know. But now he knows he's telling stories. I'm glad he's over the hump."

"Well, it's nice that you trust him with the baby. He's worried about that, you know."

Inez laughed. "I've known Edgar all my life and he's always been a sweet man. He wouldn't hurt a fly."

"Just keep telling him that."

"And Verla's finished the snowflake blanket. It's so bright the baby probably won't be able to sleep. She's started on socks now. They look like size twelve E. But she's as happy as a clam. Do you think she's over the hump, too?"

"I hope so, although she may have lapses occasionally. But I'm pleased so far." Janet busied herself with things that didn't need doing. "Inez, we may have to…you know, cancel the rest of the summer guests."

"I know, and I've thought about it a lot this morning. You and I could do it, Janet. It wouldn't be the same without Bea, but we could do it. I'm a pretty good cook and I can clean as good as the next."

"I know we could, but…I don't know." She was making it all harder by even entertaining the possibility. And it certainly wasn't fair to Inez to hold out any hope.

"Janet, we have to do it. If we close Crow's Rest, it'll take the heart right out of Bea. Even if she doesn't come back, her knowing it's here will keep her going."

Janet bent to hug the girl. If Inez could be so positive, then Janet would have to quit wallowing in her self-pity and get with it. "You know something? You are absolutely right. We'll just have to convince that stubborn son of hers that this is where Bea belongs."

"Right!" Inez cried, a victory fist held high in the air.

Three days passed before they heard anything from Little Rock, by which time Janet was a basket case. She picked up the phone a hundred times to call, but put it back down after dialing the first number. In some way she was afraid to call, afraid the news would be bad, afraid Lucas would tell her Bea was settled in a nice apartment, afraid he would tell her to begin the long process of closing Crow's Rest. Afraid his voice would be distant, without the teasing, without the promise of tomorrow. She knew if she talked to Lucas, they would argue. She would demand he bring Bea home, he would set his heels and refuse.

The warm spring days stretched toward the hot days of summer. She snatched up the phone every time it rang, and finally one morning she heard Bea on the other end. "Bea, how are you?"

"I'm fine, dear. How is Inez?"

"A different person. You wouldn't believe it. And little Beatrice is growing like a weed." There was a long pause as she waited for some reaction to the name. None came. "Well, what have the doctors said?"

"Oh, they talk in riddles, but I'm on some kind of new medicine, some beta-something-or-other."

Janet heard the false note of cheeriness in Bea's voice. "Are you out of the hospital?"

"Oh, yes. I'm with Lucas. I still have a few more tests to endure. Are things all right up there?"

"Things are just fine. Edgar is so taken with little Beatrice he's almost neglecting the garden. Verla is doing just great. The lady who was lost in Oklahoma finally got here, and Inez and I are carrying on. We miss you."

"Oh, it's such a relief to know that things are going on. It somehow makes me feel better."

Janet wanted to ask the question, wanted to know, but was afraid to know. "I guess Lucas is all right."

"Oh, I suppose. He's been in such a swivet, I hardly know. He's been rushing around here and there and going to his office. The boy is behaving in a most peculiar manner. I suppose it's the strain and all."

"I'm sure it is." What she was sure of was that he was rushing around making arrangements for Bea. "Well, tell him we said hello."

"I will, dear. And thank you, Janet, for everything."

"Get well, Bea." She walked slowly back to the kitchen to tell Inez the latest news, which wasn't any news at all. Janet smiled when she saw Inez stroking Clarence and lecturing him on his muffin-stealing behavior.

"Janet?"

Janet turned to see the new guest, a young woman named Allison, hurrying toward the kitchen. "What can I do for you?"

"Well, I wanted to go to Eureka Springs today. Could you tell me the best way to get there?"

Janet went to the reception desk and pulled out her maps, although she had little hope that they would help. Poor Allison's sense of direction was so awful, she could hardly find her way to her room. They would probably never see her again. "Just go out the driveway, turn left, when you get to the dead end, turn left again. It will take you right into town."

"Left, then left again. Surely I can't get lost with something *that* simple."

"You'll be fine." She started to suggest the woman leave a trail of breadcrumbs but held her tongue. Allison would no doubt call from Huntsville or Harrison or somewhere late that night for directions home.

Temporarily at a loss for anything to do she retreated to the garden. She felt better if she stayed busy. Edgar was busy with his hoe.

"These old weeds just about got ahead of me, Miz Janet."

"Well, you've had other things to do." She bent over and started pulling the larger weeds. The lettuce and radishes were up, but they seemed to be disappearing rapidly in a carpet of weeds.

"I swear, that baby's about the cutest thing I ever saw. I think I'm gonna start making her some wooden toys next week."

"She'd like that, Edgar."

"Miz Janet, is Bea gonna come back?"

"I don't know, Edgar, I just don't know."

"Well, it'd be a real shame if she didn't. She belongs here, you know."

Janet nodded and worked on in silence. It seemed that everyone but Lucas knew where Bea belonged. Edgar went to check on the baby, and she hoed and pulled weeds in the hot sun, letting her mind drift to the day she and Lucas and Edgar had planted the garden. It seemed so long ago.

"It's finished."

She sat back on her heels at the sound of Pete Bradley's voice. He carried a large framed picture. She stood up and brushed the dirt off her jeans. "Can I see it?"

"Sure."

He turned the painting toward her, and she sucked in her breath and held it. It was beautiful. Crow's Rest lay bathed in soft translucent watercolor. The artist had captured the essence of the place, both past and present. "Oh, Bea will love it." If she ever gets to see it, Janet thought with a stab of pain.

"Uh, I did a little something else, too." He handed her a small matted pen and ink of Edgar, sitting in the porch swing.

"That's lovely. Edgar will be beside himself. Thank you."

He scuffed at the dirt. "I feel bad about what I said that day. Edgar's great. I guess we're all scared of ending up...you know. I thought a lot about what you said, and you were right. So I thought maybe I could make it up...to you and to him."

She reached up and pecked him on the cheek. "That's the nicest thing I've heard in a long time."

"Well, I guess I'll be moving on tomorrow. But I'd like to come back next summer."

"Anytime." Darned if she would tell him they probably wouldn't be here next summer. They went in and hung the painting over the fireplace. It looked just as good as Bea had predicted. Unable to resist, she called Bea. Lucas answered the phone. "Hi," she said in a weak voice. Her heart had started racing when he said hello.

"Hi." His voice sounded far away.

"Uh, how are you?"

"Fine. How are you?"

"Busy." She searched for something to say, other than what she wanted to say. "And you?"

"Busy."

She heard the strain in his voice and decided to plunge ahead. After all, what did she have to lose? "I just wanted to let Bea know that the painting is done and up over the fireplace. It's really nice." She took a deep breath. "Darn it, Lucas, when are you bringing Bea home? She belongs here, not down there in some—some glass and brick cage playing cards with a bunch of old biddies. Inez is well now and showing a real flair for running this place. And Edgar is having the time of his life taking care of little Beatrice and . . . and Verla is crocheting socks for the baby and they're awful, but according to Bea and Inez her socks have always been awful, and—"

"Janet!"

"What?"

"Calm down."

"I'm calm." So why were her palms sweating?

"Mom's going back for her final checkup tomorrow morning. Then we'll see. But right now, I—I just don't know."

"Then you're the only one who doesn't know. Why don't you talk to her?" She could almost see him standing there stiff as a ramrod, bristling at her demands.

"I have talked to her. I have some hard decisions to make and if you think they're easy, then you're dead wrong. They're not."

"Yes they are. Just bring her home. That ought to be easy enough." *And come back with her, Lucas,* she wanted to add.

"Right. I'll tell Mom about the painting."

"Okay."

"Bye."

"Bye." She hung up, angry with herself that she had lost it and started demanding things. He was not the kind of man who took kindly to that sort of thing. Maybe she would drive to Little Rock and kidnap Bea. That would settle things once and for all. How could she possibly have fallen in love with a man as stubborn as Lucas?

TWO DAYS LATER Janet and Inez were preparing tea for Allison, who had managed to find her way home, and a new artist whom Pete Bradley had sent. He wanted to paint Crow's Rest, too, and Janet had visions of paintings hanging in every room. Little Beatrice slept in her carry seat on the table under the watchful eye of Clarence. Bea's final checkup had been yesterday and neither Lucas nor Bea had called, so the mood was not the brightest. Both women assumed Bea was staying in Little Rock and Lucas was too chicken to call and tell them.

"Everything's ready, Janet."

"Let's do it. Are our guests ready?"

"Ready and waiting. They think high tea is the cat's meow." Inez picked up the tea tray and carried it into the sitting room. Janet followed with the tray of goodies.

Janet had just poured tea and passed the scones when she saw Scooter race down the hall. Probably a drop-in. Word of Crow's Rest was getting around and people stopped by to see if they had a vacancy. She heard the front door open and started to get up. Then she heard Bea's voice.

"Lucas, dear, of course we're in time for tea. You may think the girls have abandoned tea, but of course they wouldn't. After all, it's what makes the place."

Janet collapsed back into her chair as Bea steamed into the room, Lucas behind her. He wore snug white Levi's and a striped polo shirt, just as he had that first day. Her heart pounded and she seemed unable to get out of the chair. "Bea!" she gasped in a strangled voice as she jumped to her feet.

"Hello, dears." Bea hugged Janet and Inez and sat down. "Inez, those scones look absolutely perfect."

"Thank you." Inez blushed.

"Where is our baby?"

"Sleeping in the kitchen," Inez replied.

Bea settled on the sofa. "In that case we won't disturb her. There will be plenty of time to spoil her." She poured tea for herself and Lucas.

He leaned against the wall and looked at Janet. She could read nothing in his eyes and tried to concentrate on what was being said.

"Lucas, dear, try a scone. They're every bit as good as mine."

"Umm, you're right." He ate the scone and stared at Janet.

Janet felt her scone turn to stone in her stomach. Why didn't he say something? Why didn't he do something? She wasn't sure how much longer she could sit there under that unreadable stare. She finally stood on shaky legs and tried to smile. "I'll get some more tea."

Lucas was beside her, his hand gripping her arm. "Would you folks excuse us?"

Janet felt herself being dragged out the front door and down to the boat dock. She hurried to keep up, fearing that this time he really *was* going to drown her. When their feet touched the dock, he stopped and turned to her.

"God, I've missed you." He held her face in both hands, stroking, caressing.

"You have?" She felt the fire begin to burn.

"I tried to forget, tried to tell myself you were wrong about Mom, tried to go back to work."

"You did?"

"I love you, Janet Gallen."

"You do?" His lips brushed hers. "You *do*?"

"I do. I want to spend the rest of my life with you."

"You do?" Her legs threatened to collapse as his arms encircled her.

"Janet, you've got to do something about your conversations. They lack a certain . . . scintillation. Is that a word?"

"What happened?" She virtually melted against him.

"What happened about what?" He pushed her away and sat her down on a bench. "I can't think with you that close."

"I can't spend the rest of my life with you. You're in Little Rock, I'm here." She thought that was a silly thing to say to a man who'd just said "I love you," but she was so full of questions, she couldn't think of anything else to say.

"Ah, but I'm not in Little Rock, I'm here."

"You are?" He was speaking in riddles again, or she was hearing in riddles.

"I am. I quit my job. I discovered I liked being a law judge about as much as I liked tax law. I guess I'm just a windmill tilter at heart, and there certainly seem to be a lot of windmills around here. I'm going into a law firm here with a buddy I went to law school with. And I'm going to start a small marina for sailboats, and I'm going to marry you."

Janet's head reeled. "You are? When did you decide all this?"

He leaned over and kissed her, gentle and sweet as the morning dew. "The first day I saw you. I just wouldn't admit it. Fought it like a tiger. Did all the things I used to do to prove I couldn't possibly be happy back home."

"The cow?"

He nodded. "And the garden. Except instead of proving it wouldn't work, it just whetted my appetite for more. You fit this place so perfectly, I want to enjoy it with you."

"And Bea?"

"That was the worst. Oh, I knew I was right on that one. But after three weeks of Mom rearranging everything in my apartment a hundred times and talking about nothing but this place every time I took her to the retirement home to meet other people, well, what could I do? I guess I finally understand what she needs and wants. Thanks to you." He crossed the distance between them and took her in his arms. His kiss was sweet and gentle. "Well, are you going to marry me?"

"When?"

"Right away."

She wound her arms around his neck. "Oh, Lucas, I do love you." She had never been so happy in her whole life. His kisses became more demanding and she felt herself being swept up and away.

He laughed. "We're making progress. Six words all at once. Let's go tell Mom. Although you know? I think she knew about us before I did?"

They walked to the house, hand in hand, laughing like children. "I think we'll build our house on the dogwood hill," he said.

"And we'll have a room for the white rabbit and a great big looking glass."

"What on earth are you talking about now?" He stopped to kiss her.

As his lips descended to hers, she murmured, "It's a long story. I think I'll save it for our kids." Behind his back she raised a victory fist toward the house and silently said, "Thanks, bunny."

EPILOGUE

JANET NAILED the new sign, painted by the last artist guest they'd had, to the posts and stood back to admire it.

Crow's Rest Bed and Breakfast
Catering to Older Adults

She'd wanted to add For Those of Us Who Are Forgetful, but Lucas thought it might be a little much.

She started into the house then stopped when she saw Lucas coming through the brightly cloaked autumn woods from the new house site. Construction had started, and she was so excited she could hardly stand it. She loved poring over house plans and magazines until the wee hours each night. "How do you like it?" She pointed at the sign. She saw with a sinking feeling it was crooked. He took her hammer and fixed it.

"You've been in the sailboat too much this summer. Everything you do is starting to lean." He kissed her on the cheek, ignoring the swat she gave him.

"I didn't want an editorial on the sign hanger, I wanted an opinion of the sign. I still think we should have been a little more specific."

"Not to worry, sweet. Word is already getting around."

"Don't I know it? Edgar is beside himself. Mr. Hudson worked for the Louisville Nashville or some such railroad, bless his heart. I don't think he remembers a thing after 1940. Edgar is an absolute wonder, you know. He's working with Mr. Hudson every day, dragging him back to the present and actually keeping him there for longer and longer periods. Mrs. Hudson loves it here. She'd about given up ever having another vacation." Although Edgar and Verla were no longer a problem in terms of younger guests, they had all decided that they had something more to offer to the world than just another bed and breakfast. They had begun catering to older couples where one spouse had a small memory problem. It had succeeded beyond their wildest expectations. And Inez had turned into a fine cook and was well on her way to becoming a fine manager. "And between Verla and that new Mrs. Wakely, well, I think we could build a circus tent out of snowflakes and afghans. And Verla is quite a tiger when it comes to telling people what medicine they should or shouldn't take."

He pulled her close and gently kissed her. "'Tis a fine thing we've done here, Mrs. McNair."

"It is, isn't it, Mr. McNair?"

"Oh, there you are, dears." Bea bustled out onto the porch. "Janet, could you spare a minute? I really don't know what to do. Mrs. Wakely has decided that Clarence is her first husband come back as a cat. She's got poor Clarence pinned in a corner, demanding he talk to her, since it appears he never talked to her the first time around. Clarence is quite put out by the whole thing.''

Janet and Lucas grinned at each other, holding their laughter for a later time. It wasn't the image of Mrs. Wakely that inspired the desire to laugh, it was the image of Clarence, pinned down and ''quite put out.'' ''Come on, windmill tilter, we have to save Clarence. This place can't possibly survive without the Cheshire cat.''

Harlequin Romance®

Coming Next Month

Available in May wherever paperback books are sold, or
through Harlequin Reader Service:

In the U.S.
901 Fuhrmann Blvd.
P.O. Box 1397
Buffalo, N.Y. 14240-1397

In Canada
P.O. Box 603
Fort Erie, Ontario
L2A 5X3

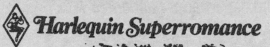

Harlequin Superromance

Here are the longer, more involving stories you have been waiting for... Superromance.

Modern, believable novels of love, full of the complex joys and heartaches of real people.

Intriguing conflicts based on today's constantly changing life-styles.

Four new titles every month.
Available wherever paperbacks are sold.

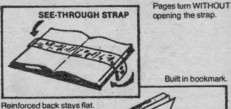